THE
ILLUSTRATED
COLONIALS
Saratoga
Book Three
BY TOM DURWOOD
A deeply intriguing, ambitious historical fiction series.
- The Prairie Review
Gorgeously written ... the author has done his research. The characters are clever, self-driven, and unique.
These books are sure to spark curious minds.
- Kerri Irish, ComfyReader book blog

Published by the Empire Studies Press

www.empirestudies.com

ISBN The Illustrated Colonials Book Three: Saratoga ebook 978-1-952520-18-1

ISBN The Illustrated Colonials Book Three: Saratoga print 978-1-952520-19-8

Artwork credits

Front cover illustration and illustrations pages 70, 74 copyright @ 2021 by Timothee Mathon.

Archival woodcut page 2. Source: Wikimedia Commons. Color by Javelin Studios.

Map page 5 by Jason Juta.

Illustrations pages 9, 24, 94 copyright @2017 Shahab Serwaty

Illustrations pages 40, 51, 52 copyright @2021 Mai Nguyen.

Illustration page 62 copyright @2021 Cristina Pritelli

Illustrations pages 14, 59, 85, 97, 113 copyright @2021 J. Ramsey

Illustrations pages 33, 41, 73, 101, 105 copyright @ 2021 Jose Luis Segura

Illustrations pages 21, 29, 82, 91 copyright @2021 Doug Lobo. Color by Javelin Studios.

Illustrations pages 11, 37, 65 copyright @2021 Sy Gardner

Illustrations pages 12, 18, 66, 89, 117 copyright @2021 Karin Wittig.

Illustration pages 16, 45, 71, 84, 112 copyright @ 2017 Victorin Ripert.

Illustration pages 26, 102, 107, 109 by Herman Rietema.

Illustration pages 43, 47, 56 copyright @ 2021 Lorenzo Natale

Illustrations pages 19, 75 copyright @ 2021 Jessica Taylor.

Illustration page 125 copyright @ 2021 Jessica Taylor. Color by Javelin Studio.

Archival decorations pages 50, 117. Source: Wikimedia Commons

Flags appearing on pages 78, 80, 121, 123. Source: Wikimedia Commons

This book is dedicated to my parents.

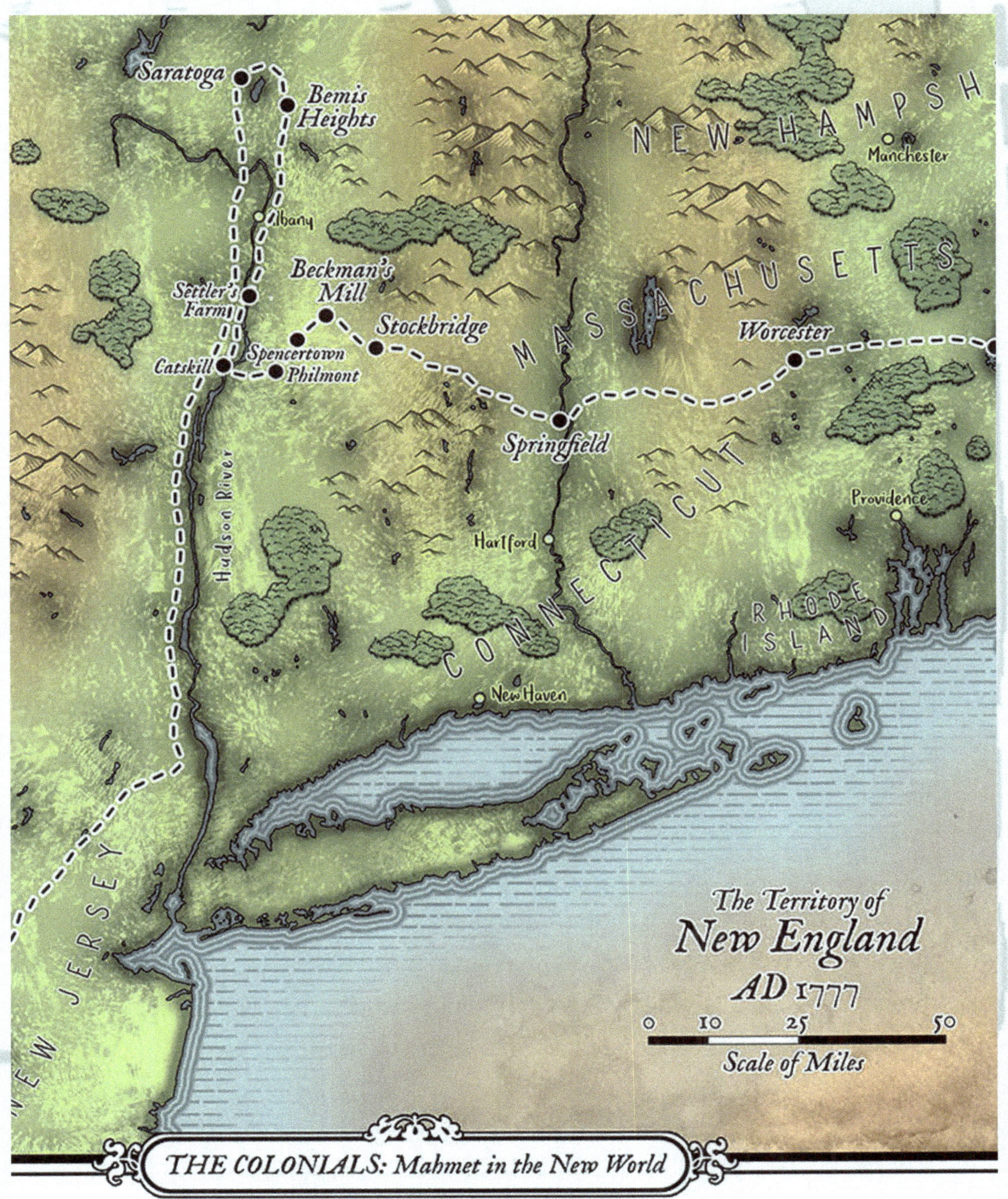

Saratoga
Bemis Heights
NEW HAMPSH
Manchester
Albany
Beckman's Mill
MASSACHUSETTS
Settler's Farm
Stockbridge
Worcester
Spencertown
Catskill
Philmont
Springfield
Hudson River
CONNECTICUT
Providence
Hartford
RHODE ISLAND
New Haven
The Territory of
New England
AD 1777
0   10   25   50
Scale of Miles
NEW JERSEY
THE COLONIALS: Mahmet in the New World

Foreword

FOR GENERATIONS, YOUNG AMERICANS HAVE been introduced to the Revolutionary War by Ether Forbes classic, *Johnny Tremain*. Penned in 1943, the novel features an apprentice who experiences personal hardship, forms a lasting bond with a friend, and finds fulfillment by joining the colonial resistance to Great Britain. It's a good story—as far as it goes.

In recent years, historians have broadened the selection of Revolutionary players and expanded the Revolution's stage. The cast now includes women, African Americans (enslaved and free), Native Americans, and colonials of all stripes. Further, the stage now stretches across the globe—challenges to the British Empire in Europe, Africa, and Asia, spurred by the Revolution unfolding in North America.

How can we introduce young readers to these new and expansive views of the American Revolution?

Thomas Durwood has found a way. In *The Colonials*, adopting but widening the *Johnny Tremain* template, he features six diverse protagonists who face adversity in curious ways, form lasting bonds with each other, and join the fight against Empire—not only the British Empire, but oppression in their own countries as well. The cast is diverse: Jaiyi Mei Ying from China, Prince Mahmoud from the Ottoman Empire (now Turkey), Sheyndil from Russia, Leo from Germany, Will O. from Holland, and Gilbert from France. Although each, in his or her way, is a misfit at home, they come together in common cause—a cause that will reshape the world.

At the unique "School for Young Monarchs" in the Alsace-Lorraine, these wayward youngsters, who push and pull and tease as teenagers do, are exposed to ideas of the Enlightenment—serious food for thought. Quick learners, they pick up innovative techniques of industry, agriculture, and commerce. They are also exposed to a political philosophy that is spreading among educated elites in Europe—and, better yet, taking root among all classes in America. There, disgruntled colonists are upset at being taxed without having any say in the matter. They insist that a government can rule only by "the consent of the governed"—a message that will resonate with oppressed people far and wide.

What can our crew of six do to support this worthy cause? That's where their adventures begin—in America and elsewhere. Readers, beware: you are in for a romp across the globe. The story is wild, but there's reason for this madness. Historically, youthful Americans have been presented with a limited view of our Revolutionary War, as if it were our business alone. But as this book suggests, powerful themes of the Declaration of Independence—liberty, equality, and "consent of the governed"—resonated throughout the world.

Fast forward a few years, when readers of *The Colonials* encounter histories of other nations in college or as adults. Foreign nations and cultures will not feel quite so "foreign" to them. They might or might not recall the particulars of Durwood's plot, but the characters will reside within them, as will the cause to which they had all pledged their allegiance.

—Ray Raphael, author of *People's History of the American Revolution*; *Founding Myths: Stories that Hide Our Patriotic Past*; *Founders: The People Who Brought You a Nation*, and seven other books on the Founding Era. Raphael is also an associate editor of *Journal of the American Revolution.*

Contents

THE ILLUSTRATED COLONIALS
Saratoga Book Three

BY TOM DURWOOD

ILLUSTRATED BY

Sy Gardner
Lorenzo Natale
Timothee Mathon
Mai Nguyen
Cristina Pritelli
John Ramsey
Jose Luis Segura
Shahab Serwaty
Jessica Taylor
Karin Wittig

The Story So Far ...

We last saw our six young 'colonials' as they faced profound changes in their families and their homelands.

Having learned the hard truth of Dubin's warning – that these ideas of liberty and equality can bring unexpected consequences – the six resolve to aid the global cause of brotherhood and natural rights, no matter the cost.

Mahmoud risks the most. Disinherited by his father, Mahmoud crosses the Atlantic. Transformed from a 'roly-poly prince' into a lean, tough-minded rifleman (and military historian), Mahmoud lands in Boston, He seeks to deliver documents of finance and alliance to Gilbert, who serves at General Washington's side. Two men follow his trail: his protector, Kace; and the assassin, Taquin.

Along the way Mahmoud meets an Iroquois brave, Gentleman Johnny Burgoyne, and the Virginian Daniel Morgan, with whom he shares Leo's rotating-bullet design. Book Three is largely Mahmoud's story.

In Amsterdam, Will implements innovative models of syndicated financing which he read in the school archives. With the Navigators' capital and Johannes' guidance, Will buys out his family's business. He leverages funds to build a network of maritime agents to give military and logistical support to the impoverished American nation. Even more significantly, he is able to finance Shay's far-reaching gambit – one that gathers alliances with Dutch merchants, Catherine the Great, the Ottoman Admiralty, and Chinese seafaring cartels.

The trilogy reaches its climax at the Battle of Saratoga, where lessons from military history and a case of mistaken identity lead to a surprising outcome.

PART ONE

The New World

You have never considered what manner of men are these Athenians with whom you will have to fight, and how utterly unlike yourselves. They are revolutionary, equally quick in the conception and in the execution of every new plan; while you are conservative—careful only to keep what you have, originating nothing, and not acting even when action is most necessary – they are bold beyond their strength. They run risks which prudence would condemn; and in the midst of misfortune they are full of hope ...

-- Thucydides, A History of the Peloponnesian War

CHAPTER 1
Nitidus' Crossing

In order to act, you must be somewhat insane.
A reasonably sensible man is satisfied with thinking.

-- Georges Clemenceau

BY THE TIME THEY REACHED the mid-Atlantic, Mahmoud had lost a considerable weight.

He hated the food.

He hated the constant motion.

He liked his duties as the Navigator's mate, and he had proved his value on more than one occasion, so the seamen tolerated him. The navigator, a Portuguese, was so eccentric, and spoke in such loops, that the crew came to prefer consulting with the Mate.

The German ship, *Jungfrau*, surged in the strong wind, pressing at a rapid clip across the Atlantic beneath rain-clouded skies.

Belowdecks, the Portuguese woke the young Turk.

"Oh, Pilot likes the speed," said the Portuguese. "But he won't like the destination. No no, he will not overly enjoy the destination ..."

The navigator, who was half-mad, had private names for the currents which criss-crossed the North Atlantic, mysterious names like *belasica* and *ohruzad*. He would greet the currents, and bid them farewell, as the ship moved westward. The Captain wanted to

take advantage of these currents as long they took him in a westward direction, towards his destination: the Portuguese advised the Captain in most colorful terms to avoid succumbing to the temptation to ride with certain currents. *Not Belasica*, he would warn, *she will betray you, in the end* ... The Portuguese would recommend that the *Jungfrau* stay with a current he liked, even if it took them off-course, rather than succumb to one of the ones he feared. To confuse matters, he had lately raised the specter of 'apparent winds,' which every pilot fears: these are quirks of ocean current and wind that distort a ship's perception of its own speed, and conspire to give the illusion of forward motion when there is none. The German captain, puzzled by the navigator's strange theories and odd language, had learned to consult with the navigator's mate, the quiet Turkish boy whose calculations always proved dependable, and whose German was flawless.

"Wind begets wind," the navigator chortled now, hearing the wind rise over the decks above them, meaning strong winds will sooner or later deliver a ship into a storm. "Best not to chase them. Oh no, best avoid that..." It seemed to Mahmoud that the Portuguese had come to completely neglect the fact that his own fate was bound to that of the pilot: any mistake the pilot made would doom the entire ship's crew. He seemed to place his entire faith in the ship itself. The *Jungfrau* was one of those sturdy, Dutch-built merchant ships. The Portuguese often referred to the Dutch shipwrights as dependable men whose skills would bring them back safely, and frequently wished that the *Jungfrau's* pilot was not German but Dutch, for "Dutchmen sail prudently, with shortened sail," and implore the protection of St. Nicholas as they travel.

"Wait! Wait!" cried the Portuguese now, crouching in the below-decks quarters like a cat. "What decides he now? Is it a lee bow?" They could feel a slight shift in the floor's pitch. "Does he luff ...? Does he seek to shake sweet *Belasica* now? Too late, *hee hee*, too late. Feel that, Mahmoud? She yaws, but she does not pitch – good girl, good girl. Let us go and help her survive this squall -- "

Mahmet and the Portuguese climbed the ladders and emerged on the quarterdeck.

They instantly saw that the Portuguese's worst fears had been realized: the current had betrayed them. It had carried them swiftly, and in the correct direction, but it had delivered them to the looming maw of an Atlantic gale. Massive dark clouds rose above the *Jungfrau*'s sails, and a biting rain swirled crazily about the decks. Mahmoud had never seen a ship's deck tilted so steeply, or waves as giant as those which rose and fell violently towards them.

"Hard down the helm, damn you!" The navigator dashed astern, to tend the tiller, which reeled and spun drunkenly.

"You. Turk."

A hand gripped Mahmoud's shoulder.

"Help us with the gaff -- "

It was the Bosun's mate, a hard-eyed young Dane.

If the Dane's tone was cold, his request was nonetheless proper. A Boatswain's Mate is responsible for the ship's rigging. A ship's crew drills endlessly, practicing the procedures for a storm. It was the responsibility of all Second Mates, including the Navigator's Mate, to help maintain the integrity of the sails and their lines.

The winds which preceded the gale were fast-changing, inconsistent in both speed and direction. The gaff sail had become badly twisted: if they could not untangle it, they would have to cut it down and raise a new one, an easy task in port but far less so in a

high wind, riding the sickening troughs and crests of twenty-foot waves. They were caught in a new, crazy rhythm, as the *Jungrfrau* skimmed down slopes of the endless breakers and caught in the waves' troughs with a nauseating lurch.

The Dane drew a prepared mizzen-line around his torso, snug under his shoulders, and crawled out onto the gaff boom, a round wood column attached to the mast which swung horizontal to the deck. Mahmoud tied a sheet around

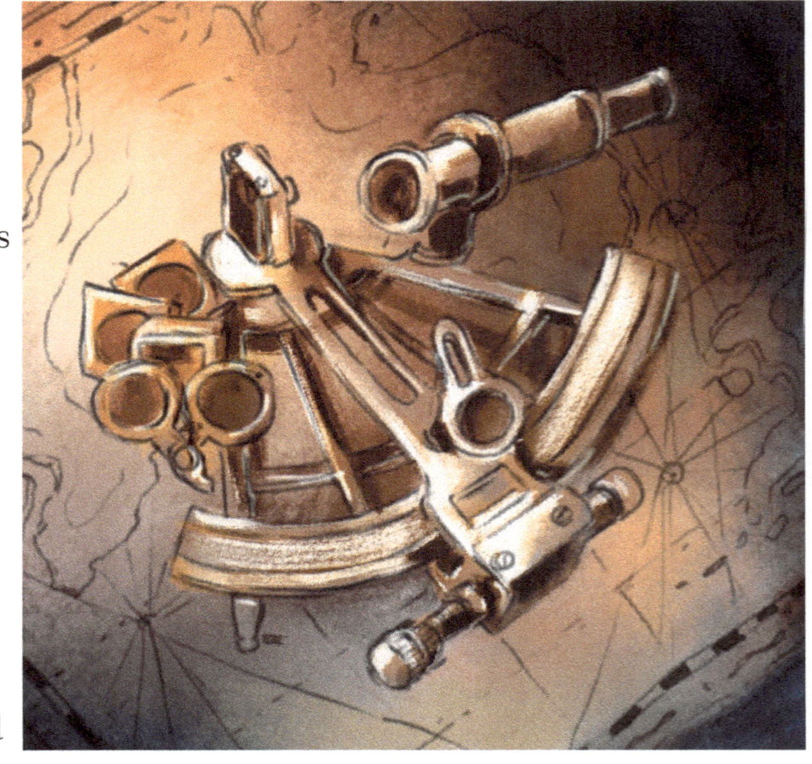

himself and clipped the sheet to the mast. He followed the Dane. Both clutched the thick webbing which was on their left-hand side.

They crawled forward, inch by inch, until they reached the mizzenmast. They could see that the bottom of the gaff-sail had been badly tattered by the cross-winds, and was rendered beyond repair. They would have to replace it.

Mahmoud called back for a new sail. It was forwarded carefully, hand over hand.

The *Jungfrau* jerked badly. Both men clutched the gaff-boom tight while it swayed, extending well out over the stormy sea into the drenching sea-spray. After a sickening ride, they were back, cold and wet and panting, ready to replace the shredded sail.

The Dane smiled.

Mahmoud saw the glimmer of a knife blade in the hand of the Bosun's Mate.

The Dane despised Mahmoud for his competence, and for his aloofness. A personable young man whose manner masked a vindictive heart, the Bosun's Mate had come to dislike the Prince before they left port, and sought only the chance to kill him: this storm was his opportunity, for -- compass tattoo or not -- none can say for sure how a sailor dies in a gale. All around them, crewmen scurried to get the new sails bent and reefed. None would see the drama that played out here, far away from the officers' eyes.

Mahmoud reached for the gaff-sheet, the very line which was attached to the Bosun's Mate.

It was beyond his reach.

Now the Dane slid towards him, the deadly knife held tight in his fist.

Mahmoud ducked as a tackle sailed by, only inches from his skull.

The Ottoman once-prince jumped off the boom and grabbed at the gaff-sheet, pulling the line tight as fell back down onto the boom.

The rope slipped from its perch around the Dane's torso and came upward on him. He realized what was happening too late, and in a panic clutched at the line, but that only made it worse. The sheet was now dug tight at his neck. The Dane looked up, realizing that someone had replaced the original hemp line with manila rope: while not so durable as hemp, manila rope is stronger, and far softer, and more elastic. In a rainstorm, this was the wrong rope to use as a lifeline, for it would be too slick to stay where it was intended.

"Back!" cried the Masters-at-Arms, on the deck behind them.

"Haul him back -- "

The *Jungfrau* lurched as yet another wave jolted her. The Dane lost his grip in the webbing and flew out over the keeling hull in a pretty arc, his eyes large with fear, his hands waving, trying to get at the rope that choked off his windpipe.

"Reel him in! For God's sake --"

But the harder they pulled, the quicker he would die, for the Navigator's Mate had been the one to replace the line, and the one to tie the knot: and it was not a clove hitch, but a slip-knot. And any knot tied in a manila line would not let go easily.

With a clatter, the Dane's knife fell to the deck.

He was near, and they could each hear his bestial curses. As he died, the Bosun's Mate knew who had murdered him.

A mountainous wave sent them sprawling.

When they looked up next, they saw the body of the Dane hanging limp, his neck snapped.

The crew looked up at the dark figure of the Navigator's mate, standing legs apart for balance. There were shadows over his eyes, and several of the superstitious seamen would later describe him as an avenging spirit, a sort of dark vindicator, or Turkish version of Achilles at Troy, standing ghostly grim over his downed foe. The Navigator's Mate ran a finger along the scar which spanned the bridge of his nose, waiting to see if the

Master-at-Arms might choose to take action. The pistol tucked in the dry space beneath Mahmoud's oilskin coat suggested that he was entirely ready, should that be the case.

As you move about in life, the once-Prince Mahmoud had once been told, some men will take to you and some will not. This matters little, for an honest man can get along, in the course of a day.

But there will be a few who hate you for no reason, and these cannot be reasoned with.

These you may have to kill.

He was learning.

There will be a few who hate you for no reason, and these cannot be reasoned with. These you may have to kill.

CHAPTER 2
Lunch with Burgoyne

Our Prince Johnny saw himself and his
own attributes in brilliant clarity,
but not so his adversary. That was his undoing.

-- Saul Dubinsky, A Brief History of Botany

MAHMOUD, THE NAVIGATOR'S MATE, STOOD on the bridge.

The Boston skyline was like nothing he had ever seen.

It was one of those fresh-scrubbed mornings on the day the *Jungfrau* tacked into Boston Harbor, approaching from the north, where the scattered sandbars force seamen to pay close attention to their charts.

She passed the deep sheltered harbors of the port of Boston and, as the wind shifted, ran parallel to the colony's long, generous coastline. They could see the many outer sand bars and islands which dotted Boston Harbor. On one of them, Rainsford Island, was a quarantine hospital, on another a poorhouse. *The Jungfrau* passed moored ships from all over the world, ships with names like *The Recovery, The Increase, The Abigail*, as well as triple-decked English warships, with their endless batteries of guns and menacing curved prows. The wooden fisherman's houses along

Dorchester's many wharves were painted in bright and friendly hues. Even the whites looked like colors. Gulls swooped down in sharp dives to grab at scraps tossed by the *Jungfrau*'s laughing crewmen.

As they drew close to Boston's Long Wharf, the navigator's mate standing at the ship's railings could see the tower of the North Church. He heard the church's bells. He saw the drawbridge at Water Street, and the sprawl of Oliver's Dock. He caught glimpses of thronged sidewalks and green commons; not the trimmed lawns of Topkapi, but parkways in an open design, were people of all walks mingled ... or was it his imagination, filling in details which his eyes could not yet see?

Kemal would be surprised at how advanced the infidels have come, he remarked to himself.

Boston was city at war, yet not a city under siege, or one in which the wartime atmosphere repressed the inhabitants' daily life. Red-coated British soldiers mixed in with shop patrons and tethered goats and running schoolchildren, who seemed to be everywhere.

The burgeoning industries of Boston's abundant fish and timber had created a wealthy class of merchants, whose stately home they could see along the waterfront, as well as shopkeepers and dealers and agents; but it was the vigorous middle class of ship's captains and mates, shipwrights, tradesmen, ropemakers, sailmakers and mechanics of many different trades who were the backbone of maritime Massachusetts. They lived in the modest, wood-framed dwellings set closely together near the waterfront, among the poulterers of Broad Street and spread into communities up and down the coast, towns with names like Newburyport, Ipswich, Salem, and Gloucester.

Standing on the *Jungfrau*'s deck as she slid over the water towards her docking, Mahmoud thought of Constantinople. It was his home, and represented all that was familiar; this was so different. Where Constantinople was freighted with history and built by long dead architects of other ages, Boston seemed new, and if equally teeming, more amiable. The Bosporus was so deep that it tended to meet the shore in cliffs: here, children waded on sand bars and sailed in tiny skiffs, while home-made docks seemed to emerge from every town and neighborhood. All the people of Boston had access to the sea, it appeared.

These were the American colonies, close enough to touch.

Somewhere, beyond those trees, walks Gilbert.

A thrill rose in Mahmoud. He touched a hand to the documents strapped beneath his jacket. At that moment, he believed that he could indeed change history: not because Sheyndil pronounced it, but because he himself believed that it was true.

The smell of spiced beef roasting over a flame wafted across the ship's bow. Mahmoud's appetite awakened. He had all but given up eating, faced with the inedible salt pork and dry biscuits of his Atlantic passage.

"Strike the sails!" called the Bosun.

Real food, imagined the young Prince.

* * *

"I beg your pardon," said the exotic young man to the table of twelve.

He wore a most unusual red jacket, one with a high collar, in the Oriental style, and bedecked in subtle, swirling celestial designs. His head and upper carriage were most still and erect, almost regal, while his knees were slightly bent and he stood on his toes, with a slight forward cant.

Gentleman Johnny Burgoyne looked up.

The table's lively hubbub quieted.

"I could not help but overhear the smallest part of your conversation," said the youth. He was of a dark complexion, tall and lithe (for Mahmoud had shed a quarter of his body weight during the Atlantic crossing).

"Might you, by any small chance," he said to the garrulous, loud-voiced gentleman at the head of the table, "be the author of a most excellent treatise on the use of light cavalry in the capture of *Valencia de Alcantra*?"

These extraordinary words hung in the clear Boston air beneath the crystal chandeliers in the air of the Porcellian Club, a dining club for the international ruling classes, a club whose chef was reputed to serve the best roast chicken in the colonies.

"I am indeed!" said a delighted John Burgoyne, author of that same treaty, slapping his hand on his knee.

"It is an honor to meet you, sir," said Mahmoud, smiling as he extended a hand in friendship. "You are the first to fully account for the Spanish campaign in Portugal. I spent a week studying it."

"If that is the case, then your schoolmaster is a cruel man indeed," laughed Burgoyne. *"Cave ab homine unius libri."*

"Bene legere saecla vincere," Mahmoud replied, and Burgoyne nearly fell off his chair with laughter.

An array of amazed faces among ruffled white shirts and red coats around the table greeted this exchange: Burgoyne's corps of officers had come from England to help the great man crush the rabble army of Continentals. From where they sat, at the formal dining table on the lush carpet of the dining club's dining room on the topmost floor of a red brick structure tucked in the crook of a Back Bay cul-de-sac, diners could view the sweeping expanse of Boston Harbor, from Charlestown on the left to Brighton on the right.

"Why, there cannot be a dozen men in the civilized world who have read it." Burgoyne stood to shake his fellow scholar's hand warmly, with both of his own.

"My publisher had to practically be *bribed* to bring it out. But now he'll hear from me -- *Haw!*"

Gentleman Johnny Burgoyne, a man who embraced all of life's moments, good and bad, downed the remnants of his wine glass and offered a goblet to his new friend.

Burgoyne, military scholar, playwright, and bon vivant, had recently returned from wintering in England to direct the campaign that would end the American rebellion. His ruddy face and reddish-brown hair contrasted sharply with the snow white of his breeches and blouse.

"Bring this young man a chair!"

"I cannot bother you, sir, I only wished to intro -- "

"Nonsense! You must sit, sir, and do me the honor of telling me through what remarkable chain of events you managed to come into the possession of that obscure paper of mine?"

With much prodding from Burgoyne, and with some degree of embarrassment, Mahmoud introduced himself, using his full name, and sat down.

"A Muslim Prince in the New World. What wonders may we yet see," exclaimed Burgoyne. "And was it an Ottoman school where you studied my little exercise?"

"The Academy at Selestat," replied Mahmoud, realizing too late that this was the wrong answer to give.

"I know it not, but it must be a most enlightened school indeed," said Burgoyne, although he did know it. "And what brings you to the colonies, Prince?"

"I will take a month to observe the American experiment, as the French writers do. To see if there is aught of value for my own people."

"There is plenty of value in America, I can attest," nodded Burgoyne. "But the singular lesson your Turkish folk need to know is this: obey the King's law – in your case, young highness, the *Caliph*'s law – or suffer the consequences." He lifted a glass, and his companions immediately raised a chorus of seconds and huzzahs. *"Redde Caesari quae sunt Caesaris.* The punishment is most harsh!" Burgoyne's junior officers called out "Hear, hear" and "What, what" at these stirring words. Several more declarations (and responses) in this same vein followed.

"Are you writing any new works?" asked Mahmoud. "I thought you might have opinions on the tactics at Quebec."

"No. No writings of recent, I'm afraid. BUT," said Gentleman Johnny loudly, with an eye to his young companions, "but I announce to you, young Sultan, right here and right now, that I fully intend to conduct a campaign that will be written about FOR MANY WARS TO COME." This brought renewed cheers. "We mean to actually *fight* the war this time round." He toasted the sentiment. *"Parry* the rebels' cowardly raids, *lure* them out in the open for a *proper* battle, *deliver* them a decent hiding. SACK the cities. KILL the leaders." This engendered a brief round of singing, and several of the young Englishmen stood, hands to hearts, as if in the presence of royalty. "By God," continued Burgoyne, "once Thomas *Jefferson* and George *Washington* and -- who are the others? -- yes, *Paine* and *Franklin* and *Adams*, once the rebel leaders are swinging from the lamp-poles of Harvard Square, we shall have an understanding. War is war. Good lord. Sedition is sedition."

War is war. Good lord. Sedition is sedition.

"*De Jure Belli ac Pacis*," commented Mahmoud, smiling as he spoke. "'To deprive another of what belongs to him, merely for one's own advantage, is repugnant to the law of nature,'" he quoted, although he did not particularly believe it.

"My dear young Sultan, you must join my staff!" exclaimed Burgoyne, delighted. "This minute! I will make you a corporal within the month. Not one of my staff can quote Grotius, and appropriately, too. I insist upon it! You will chronicle my victories, and set my American campaign in the pantheon of battles, alongside Marathon and Carthage. We carry with us the best wine in the colonies!"

This statement set off a new round of cheering. Mahmoud took advantage of the ensuing hubbub to decline Burgoyne's generous offer and take leave of the gracious host, who, as Mahmoud left, managed to give him a parting piece of advice:

"The colonials, while admirable, are amateurs at war, and will not be able to withstand what is coming. Do not tarry too long among them, my Prince, lest you become part of their tragedy … "

* * *

The loyalist, a British spy in the employment of General John Burgoyne, hid himself cleverly from the young Ottoman's line of sight.

He followed Mahmoud as he walked through Faneuil Hall and Quincy Market, and out along the planks and gables of the Long Wharf.

It was an easy task, for the youth did not imagine he was being followed.

Gentleman Johnny Burgoyne had not been so drunk that he had not recognized the name of the Academy at Selestat as the same school at which Jean Frestel had taught, the same academy attended by the young French noble, Gilbert du Motier. Nor had he been drunk enough to miss the small henna tattoo on the Prince's wrist.

Immediately upon Mahmoud's exit from the dining club, Burgoyne had assigned two of his young officers to trail the Ottoman Prince, while he summoned the loyalist, who soon enough replaced the more conspicuous redcoats. "I have no intention of allowing a healthy young royal with colonial leanings and an encyclopedic knowledge of military history wander about the rebel territories," Burgoyne had announced, to which comment his sycophants sniggered and proposed a toast to Gentleman Johnny.

The loyalist spy followed Mahmoud as he wandered onto the commons. The youth seemed to marvel at the broad parkway, a combination of a park and boulevard: he took a seat on one of the benches which line the Commons and watched the parade of humanity beneath the shaded paths beneath arching elms. Every third person seemed to carry one of the distinctive flat-bottomed bags with leather handles and straps at the top.

He took interest in a pair of girls his own age, and the girls noticed him as well.

He listened to the speakers on the Commons, who inveighed from elevated platforms.

The loyalist spy followed his Turkish guest down Atlantic Avenue, where the ponies that pull the soap carts warn you of their coming with ringing bells around their necks. He dawdled by the tethered goats while Mahmoud got his long hair cut at a barber's, and fed the pigeons, and bought a sensible jacket and breeches so he might better fit in among the Bostonians. He paused to admire his own reflection in the clothier's window.

It was not until he overheard the youth ask for directions to the Cambridge offices of the Dutch shipping agent, Mickler Sykes, that the spy took action. Burgoyne had warned him this might happen, and had given the King's loyalist three very emphatic instructions: One, *Carry him north, to Canada; before you let him go*; two, *Let him see none of his captors*; and, three, *Do him no harm He bears the Navigators' mark.*

CHAPTER 3

A Carriage Ride

What was given to us is stripped away.
What remains is what we have earned.

-- Saul Dubinsky

I'M MOVING.

Deep in the forest of night, young Mahmoud, Lesser Prince of the Ottoman Kingdoms -- known in this new land as Nitidus Smith -- rose from the bench seat.

Mahmoud could hear the clopping of a team of horses.

He was sitting in a moving carriage.

I need to get these letters to Gilbert.

He swore long and emphatically. He rubbed his nose, where it had been broken in the shipyard fight, to remind himself that he had survived deadly things before.

What if I am too late -- ?

He had to get out of here – wherever this was.

Fast horses were pulling a carriage along a smooth road in a forest, and he was inside the carriage.

He could feel leather upholstery beneath him. He put his hand out to touch the windows: there were steel bars across them.

As his senses returned he was suddenly aware of a colossal thirst. He found three corked bottles

strapped upright, tucked in the cushions, in a corner and drank one of them dry. The water was sweet.

His head hurt. He winced and reached back to feel a tender welt, heavily bandaged, where he had been struck.

Who did this?

He looked out the barred windows and could now make out   rushing by

Where am I? How far have we gone?

It was a road coach, one of the heavy closed wagons you see traveling between cities, a coach-and-four by the sound of it. He tested the bars at the windows and discovered that they were not individual bars but part of a metal frame that encircled the entire carriage, walls, floor and roof: this was a prison-coach, adapted from its original use so it could ferry prisoners between prisons.

His pack was on the seat beside him. The knife had been taken from his belt, but the letters strapped to his chest were safe, still-sealed, untouched.

These are not burglars.

He checked the hidden sash around his waist, where he carried his gold: also intact.

I have been kidnapped.

Slowly, his eyes adjusted to the darkness.

Burgoyne ...

* * *

Young men want only good things for others. Young men have generous hearts. Young men believe in themselves on a grand scale. Yet young men have no inkling of how wicked and entrenched are the forces which the world arrays against them.

A terrible melancholy fell over Nitidus. The colossal idiocy of his actions crashed down on him. He lay helpless on the shaking bench seat in the barred carriage and considered his situation. He was captive, riding in a prison cell on wheels, moving in a northerly direction on a continent at war where he was utterly unknown, unloved, without friends or family. No single soul would come to his aid. His own puffed-up thoughts and comments all came back to him now. He had thought he had been so bold and so daring, when in fact all he had done was to leave his family. Everyone he had ever met in his life lay a world away. In his pride, he had abandoned himself to fate. Now he was helpless, and no one within ten thousand leagues cared a fig whether he lived or died.

The colossal idiocy of his actions crashed down on him.

He had not counted on the strangeness.

He had assumed that America would be more or less like home, or like Alsace, only with bigger forests.

But everything was different. Even the air tasted different. The people looked different, and smelled different, and held themselves differently.

I have no place here. What am I doing?

The horses who pull this coach have a place in the world, yet I do not. They have a clear purpose. I have none.

He looked through the barred windows up at the stars. There he found familiar sights.

These are the same stars I watched with Shay, and Leo, and my sisters, from the roof of the palace …

He tapped the thick hidden belt around his waist. He recalled that this miserable life did have a purpose.

He reminded himself of his mission: the letters Clotilde needed to be placed in the hands of Gilbert.

I must find Gilbert.

Clearly, his captors had been instructed to transport him, and not to kill him. He was alive. He had hope. He recognized the stars.

He fell asleep.

* * *

This will truly be a great nation, Mahmoud could not help thinking as dawn came, *for these excellent roads seem to reach forever.*

Who builds such roads?

These colonial roads were firmly built, smooth to the eye but hilly enough to the feet. No one person derived benefit from these roads; they had been built in the thought that all would benefit. The roads bore no signs, no ownership, no tolls. The dirt was well packed, and the brush cut away ten feet back from the road, leaving no place for bandits to hide

This will be a mighty empire.

In the daylight, he looked around his little moving cage.

The heavy dray was suspended on strong braces. He felt along the surfaces of the cab's interior, and on its ceiling. There had once been a hatch in the roof.

He had welded metal in Kace's shop, as well as some of the hot-water pipes on Topkapi's roof, so he knew that any weak point would be at the seams, where two beams had been joined. Working as quietly as he could, he ripped the heavy fabric away from the walls. He tore the carpeting away from the floors until he could trace the metal bars which formed the carriage-cell's framework.

He began to kick at them, timing his blows with their passage over rocky sections of road so it would not be heard. He did not want his captors to guess his intentions.

By dawn, he had exposed a small hole in the floor.

He could see the carriage's running gear. As he studied it, he reckoned that the carriage chassis allowed the two front wheels to turn independently of the rest. What he had before him was a splinter bar; the ball at the end of the pole formed a socket for the front axle. If he jammed it down, it would retard the motion of the wheels and send the carriage skidding.

With a deadly zip, a bullet winged past him and buried itself in the leather upholstery.

"Virginians!"

He heard the panic in the driver's voice.

He stood on the gunnel.

He felt the driver yank hard on the reins.

The horses strained.

The carriage rocked.

He thrust himself to the floor.

There was a sudden crash: a splintering impact. The carriage somersaulted twice, sending him tumbling. The carriage rolled a third time and struck something and burst open. Light and color spilled into the dark little cage.

He could hear shouting and quick bangs.

The carriage rolled a third time and struck something and burst open.

A band of cloaked and buckskinned figures came towards him. Their leader, a tall man with a deep voice, spoke.

"Are ye with the colonial cause?

"Yes," replied Mahmoud.

"Can you fire a rifle?

"Yes."

The caped man seemed to have taken him in with a glance, and determined that he was one to ride the river.

He shoved a rifle into the young man's hands.

"You're with us now," he growled.

CHAPTER 4
The Battle of Beckman's Mill

Attack Attack Attack

-- Motto of the 34th Infantry Division

"THAT'S WHERE THEY WERE TAKING you, lad," said the Virginians' leader, Daniel Morgan.

The Mill at Beckman's Pond was a sprawling, sturdy stone structure three stories tall. The fortress spanned a stream, where a water wheel worked day and night, lifting liquid and turning the gears of the millstones within. Guard towers rimmed the roof. Along the flanks of the drawbridge were sluices and walkways.

"They've got a month's worth of bullets and powder stored in there. And they hold four of my men captive."

The mill sat in a clearing of the orchard beyond. It had been built over the stream, raised on stone foundations over the level terrain. They watched redcoats enter the fortress.

"We've got it surrounded. But the doors only open from within."

The Sixth Rule of War. Mahmoud could hear Master Frestel's voice. *Always remain on the Offensive. He who gives up the attack will surely lose the day.*

He knew what to do.

He circled, crouching, among the trees bordering the clearing.

The British and their loyalists were still unaware of the carriage's crash and the Virginian's attack.

He dove into the stream.

He swam through the cool water in silence, slipping beneath the moving wheel. He swam under the bubble and splash of the surface, under the rotating buckets. Emerging on the other side – inside the mill -- he grabbed onto the paddle wheel and let it lift him.

He felt the cool morning air.

He stepped onto a narrow landing along the trenches which caught the mill water and coolly walked toward doors as though he were part of the loyalist swirl. A shouting guard pointed at him, but it was too late: Mahmoud grabbed the latch and slammed against the door, flinging it open.

Morgan and his men roared into Beckman's Mill.

Mahmoud struck two redcoats who tried to stop him and jammed a wheelbarrow into the breach, so that the doors lodged open.

A young redcoat fired at him and missed. A second shot at him from the loft; the shot went wide.

In the confusion of the garrison rushing towards them, Mahmoud managed to advance. He fought his way along the perimeter until he found the twin doors at the back. He heaved the heavy bar up and, failing to free the lock, took a hatchet and splintered the door at its latch it until it gave way.

* * *

Daniel Morgan shook his head. He told the young visitor that he had acquitted himself well. He took a rifle from its wrappings and gave it to Mahmoud.

"It's the new Ferguson. Breech-loader. This is the one we've been hearing about. We'll see how Prince Johnny favors it."

"Are ye Mohican?" asked one of the Virginians of Mahmoud.

"Turk," replied Mahmoud. "I am Turkish."

"Your jacket is too big."

"I know. It was my father's."

"What is your name, boy?"

"I am Mahmoud," he said. "And I have come a long way to join your cause."

"It's a just cause," said Morgan. "We may not win this round. The British have too much for us, and most of our boys are farmers. If we can hold 'em off 'till the Fall, things might change."

"I need to find my friend," said Mahmoud. "He is a Frenchman who serves as an aide to General Washington."

"A Frenchie, advising Washington," sneered Morgan. "That sounds about right.

"Washington. He's a play actor caught in a real war," said Morgan. "This ain't no polite contest. They mean to hunt down our families, and murder our leaders. Why, some kind of assassin murdered a shop-girl in Newton two days ago.

"What is your friend's name?"

"Gilbert," answered Mahmoud. "Marie-Joseph Paul Yves Roche Gilbert du Motier. The Marquis de La Fayette," he added hopefully.

"Laffite? Is that it? Lafitte?"

"La-*fie*-yette," said Nitidus. "Lafayette."

"I have na' heerd of him," said Morgan, "but if he is with Washington then you need to head south. Washington is with the Third Army, over to Morristown. Giving out his orders."

"Laffite? Is that it? Lafitte?" asked Morgan. "La-*fie*-yette," said Nitidus. "Lafayette."

"Writing his letters," added another rifleman.

"Busy avoiding Howe," commented another.

"He should have been at Ticonderoga," said Morgan. "He avoids the fighting."

"Ticonderoga?" asked Mahmoud. "The British have taken Fort Ti --?"

"Aye. Ticonderoga fell in less than a week. And now the redcoats seek to widen the field. We have two more redcoat forts to take care of, then we rendezvous with Arnold to free Boston. Ten Broeck says that Burgoyne will turn east at Skenesborough, to secure New England."

"No, he won't," said Mahmet. "At least, I wouldn't. And Burgoyne himself hasn't, in the past. In all his battles, he stays on the offensive. He never doubles back on secured territory.

"Burgoyne treasures glory above efficiency. He wants a good story. He wants to impress his sponsors in Parliament, and defensive posturing does not help him.

"He is coming straight down the Hudson," concluded Mahmoud. "He wants Manhattan. In doing so, he will cut off New England from the rest of the colonies."

Morgan gave a low whistle.

"If what ye say is true, we need to git to Half Moon fast, and git all the militia men down to Fort Edward."

"Saratoga might be better," said Mahmoud, tracing the river's course on the map.

"Saratoga might be better," said Mahmoud, tracing the river's course on the map.

"How do I get to Morristown?"

"Show him on your map, Jem. Here. You want this road, here. It skirts Iroquois country and lies wide of the British camps."

"Where am I?"

"Brother, you're here. At the head of the Hudson Valley. That land that King George most covets."

"You're a colonial now, lad," suggested Morgan. "Find a way. Do what you must.

"Tom can give you a pack. You may want to avoid the main roads, if there is some sort of price on your head. The woods ain't much better, if you run into a band of Iroquois. Pick your poison.

"And take one of these." He tossed a long knife, in a leather sheath. "Give Gentleman Johnny my greetings if you see him afore me."

CHAPTER 5

Kace in the New World

Perelman squinted at the sky
as though contemplating something
I would never understand.

-- Brett Forrest

THE TALL, BROAD COSSACK WHO came off the Greek ship made inquiries along the Boston harborside.

He found a message at the Inn waiting for him. Here is what it read:

Another has been dispatched to welcome our friend. Beware.

Kace folded the note. He moved along the docks, making inquiries about a Turkish boy in a gaudy jacket. As he moved through the heaped crates and surging streets of the Faneuil marketplace, he understood that as urgently as he sought Prince Mahmoud in order to protect him, another man was seeking him just as urgently, in order to kill him.

This time, the henna compass tattooed on the boy's wrist would not save him.

Will I find him in time? Kace wondered.

* * *

Taquin, the assassin, disembarked.

Few took notice, for the man walking down the gangway from the Spanish ship to Faneuil markets looked like so many others.

He left the docks and mixed into the swirl of commerce.

He was fascinated by the spoon-makers, fabrics, shoes, slippers, rugs, all the alleys leading to pewter shops and silversmiths and oyster bars.

He had a kindly look, like a schoolteacher.

He had been chosen by Mahmoud's enemies not only for his inner ferocity, but for his outward manner, because he looked unlike an assassin. He would be able to travel, and to move freely among the English.

The printers and bookbinders plied their ink-stained trade. He leafed through a book on ancient Rome, and another concerning the Orient and the splendors of Mongolia.

He did not like books. People and events of the past held no interest for him. This was unfortunate: if he had, he would know that treachery is the reward most commonly reaped by those who collude with murderers.

Now, Taquin needed information.

The assassin moved among the colonials.

CHAPTER 6

Lone Trek South

Perhaps no district can furnish a livelier picture
of the cruelty and fierceness of savage warfare
than the country which lies between the
head waters of the Hudson and the adjacent lakes.

-- James Fenimore Cooper

THERE IS A BAND OF smallish monkeys – you may already know this – a band of monkeys, smallish, with grey fur and white faces, smallish nimble monkeys who live in the jungles of New Guinea (or Danish Guinea, or Papua, as it is sometimes known). When one of the members of this band of monkeys sees a snake, the he- or she-monkey will immediately call out "*Snake!*" It is a distinctive word, among monkeys, a word unlike other words in the cricking monkey tongue. The entire band then takes up the word, calling *Snake Snake Snake* to themselves, and to one another, as they agitate in the leafy trees and bounce up and down on the branches. They call *Snake* to the snake itself, as though the reptile might not know its own name, or might be unaware that the entire monkey population saw him clearly.

They use the word over and over. Sometimes, by naming a threat, we can banish it.

"

But today, Mahmoud, third son of the sixth wife of the Sultan of All Ottomans, could not name that emotion which plagued him, so he could not banish it.

It was an overwhelming feeling, and it washed over him like a wave.

None of the books on war tell you that you must survive the journey to the battlefield before you try and vanquish the enemy. Yet it is so. Minamoto at *Dan-No-Ura* and Odysseus at Ithaca and Pizarro at Cajamarca all had to live through a hejira of horrors in strange terrains before ever delivering the first blow on a level battlefield. Landscapes and seascapes– the treacherous swells of Bach Dang, the jungles of the Chindits, the wind-swept ravines of the Alps – have killed far more warriors than has any battle.

That night, a new and overpowering wave of doubt crashed into the young Prince's being, into his stomach and chest and legs and arms – this was doubt that he could even traverse this wild land and make it out alive.

He was not a Prince here.

I should give up, he thought.

I should give up right now.

He was acutely aware of how very much he did not know.

A great longing came over him, a terrible solitude, all-encompassing, as sometimes happens when we cannot surround ourselves with familiar props and faces and the comforts of certainty. Young Mahmoud wept, and felt his heart was breaking; yet he could not say why. He could not say which single emotion it was. He longed terribly for something he could not name.

I am ridiculous. Everything I do or say is stupid.

He called upon his ancestors, as he had learned to do in the mosque, and he remembered their words (which suddenly made sense). He repeated them to himself, over and over.

Too many unexpected things happened in America.

In the morning, he felt he could at least walk southward. Mahmoud did not want to linger in this strange new land, but to find Gilbert as quickly as he could, hand over the letters, and go home.

He trotted on the road heading west, towards the Hudson. He would take the river south, to New York, then cross to New Jersey, where Washington camped. He would reunite with his friend Gilbert and give him the news.

He stepped on dry sticks and made loud crackles, so he made sure to pick his way carefully.

A deer moved away at his approach.

He stopped at a pond and drank among the cat-tails, under a grove of alders. He rubbed his feet.

Now the road climbed zig-zag up through the juniper forest. He crossed a stream that fell down the hillside in a waterfall.

He came to the top of the paths, and the road straightened as it dangerously skylined along the shoulders of the mountains. He passed through sheets of fog, masses of vapor with different strata, some denser than others.

He ran among and above the craggy hills, buried in green terrain like the surface of blocks in a long-lost civilization, half-buried, its full form hidden below what we can see with our eyes.

The thick wall of trees parted and he caught a glimpse of the lordly Hudson; it was a rare sight. For all his worries over surviving it, Mahmoud was struck by the river's brooding beauty.

A herd of deer, migrating, moved in front of him, across the highlands. They saw him but did not recognize him as a danger. They were bigger and more powerful than he had imagined.

Below, he could see yellow patches of grain marked by stone walls and low wood-rail fences, the white walls of cottages. To the south, in the distance, lay the primeval contours of the eastern summits, burly palisades like a barrow piled by giants.

Above he saw a flock of birds moving south against billowing clouds and the shadow of an unrisen moon.

The British can multiply their forces all they want, thought Mahmoud, *but this land is too vast and too wild, too independent. The British may conquer the people – for now. But they will never conquer this land.*

Slowly, as he moved steadily along the river, he came under the spell of the land.

The lattices of black boughs thinned. More and more, he could see the expanse of the mighty river, here almost three miles in width.

He stopped to rub his feet.

He watched the day tumble down the mountainside and sink into sparkling night.

An owl called the watches.

Mahmoud would not be denied.

CHAPTER 7

Unity of Command

Life is not a matter of holding good cards,
but sometimes, playing a poor hand well.

-- Jack London

THE SEVENTH RULE OF WAR is this: *Unity of Command.*

For every objective, ensure unity of effort under one responsible commander.

The force which breaks this rule will tend to lose its battles. Look at Tsushima, for God's sake.

On the second morning of his trek south to find his friend Gilbert, Mahmoud was descending a steep decline which he hoped would lead him to the Hudson. He had left the road behind, cutting across one of the fields and into passable forest land. He felt sure the river was less than a day in front of him. The stars told him that he was going in the right direction, but the terrain was so irregular and the paths through it so winding and crooked, he felt lost. He emerged from the decline into a short ravine, and from the ravine into a wooded patch.

He heard a rustle.

He stopped.

He was used to the sounds of the forest now, enough to recognize the sounds of a creature in trouble.

The rustle was that of a trapped creature, perhaps a fox or a beaver caught in one of the hunters' snares. He was careful not to move a muscle. He waited a long, long time, counting his breaths to 100 before proceeding. He made his way through the underbrush, towards the sounds.

He came to a clearing.

It was an Indian brave, a youth his own age.

The boy saw Mahmoud at once.

He had been staked out, clearly left to die. Tightly-knotted rawhide thongs pinned his limbs tightly to pegs pounded in the ground: his wrists were bloody where was trying to wrest them free.

He trembled, but anger burned in his eyes, as though he had been unfairly convicted.

Mahmoud cut him free. The thongs would not give, and it took too long to cut them -- the brave seized the knife as soon as one hand was free to complete the task himself.

The brave uttered a low warning.

Mahmoud pivoted to face a warrior (where he had come from, Mahmoud could not guess). He raised one forearm to block the falling tomahawk. The brave he had freed jumped on the attacker's back and slit the warrior's throat. As the warrior fell dead, the brave nimbly grabbed the man's tomahawk and bashed his skull once, twice, three times.

"*He* won't follow us. Come on!" the brave whispered (in French). He took the dead man's knapsack.

"*Let's go --* "

They ran down the slope, finding the steepest part.

They heard noises fall in behind them – others gave chase.

"*This way!*"

The brave leapt onto a stone ledge overlooking a deep stream.

He held out his arm to keep Mahmoud from falling into the water.

They turned and moved along the ledge until they came to a rope bridge that served as a span across the roaring brook below.

As soon as Mahmoud was across, the brave cut at the rope=bridge supports until they gave way.

He handed the knife back to Mahmoud as they ran.

"Run low!"

Arrows flashed in the shrubs around them. They turned into the forest. They moved pell-mell through the underbrush. The arrows stopped. Their pursuers had no way across the brook. Not yet.

They came to a craggy cliff. Mahmoud followed the path around its base.

The brave held him and pointed up the cliffside.

"This way," he said. "Red Wolf hates to climb."

* * *

This mountain range, the range we call the Adirondacks, is unlike most others. Made from sole of the oldest rock on earth, they have been pushing upwards for fifteen million years, and are still rising, as you read this. And while most mountain ranges are various peaks in a single, connected ridgeline, these are not. Each peak in the Adirondack is its own formation, some quirk in prehistory, when some Iapetean volcano had shoved this ancient rock upwards through the earth's mantle and left the craggy juts and squared hills of the range unconnected to the others. There is no common line of high terrain, no connectivity or shared raised level; a climber must ascend and descend each peak in full. It is enigmatic.

This jagged and disordered topography made the escaping pair's climbing arduous.

They climbed straight up the cliffs (or so it seemed to Mahmoud), then, without even pausing to celebrate, trotted across the summit and descended the other side. By early afternoon, the Ottoman once-Prince was lightheaded from the heights and the unceasing motion.

They switched directions twice.

They crossed wide swaths of shale, where their steps made no marks. Twice his Iroquois companion turned to look at the canopy of forest, to gauge the progress of their pursuit.

"Huh. They have given up."

They stopped. Mahmoud almost fell over from exhaustion.

The brave opened the pouch he had taken from the dead man's jacket pocket. He passed shares of dried fish and berries to Mahmoud.

"They have other worries. These woods are filled with their enemies."

"What is your name?" asked Mahmoud.

"Atayataghronghta."

"That is too long."

"You may call me Shooting Star."

"I am Nitidus."

The brave removed a fish bone from his mouth.

"That's a terrible name."

"Better than my full name."

"No matter," said Shooting Star, helpfully.

The Iroquois spoke French like no Frenchman ever did, in a sort of singsong cadence, swooping each of the verbs, as though imitating an eccentric teacher, or perhaps mocking the language itself.

"I am Iroquois," said the brave. "Your skin is like mine, but your features are not.

"Tell me brother, what tribe are you?"

"The Turks. The Ottoman Turks."

"I do not know them." He spat out another fish bone.

"It is a tribe from across the sea."

"The sea. What sea?"

"The Atlantic."

Shooting Star considered the name. "Ah. That is far indeed."

"You are marked for death, Strange One," he said. "For helping me.

"You are marked for death, Strange One," he said. "For helping me. Don't worry, I am a mighty warrior," he added.

"Don't worry, I am a mighty warrior," he added.

"Who is chasing us?" asked Mahmoud.

"Red Wolf. A coward and a thief. The worst chieftain we have ever had."

They each took a handful of berries. They tasted impossibly sweet. Both braves drooled juice.

"He is still following us," said Shooting Star. "From below. He will guess where we are going, and wait for us.

"We've got to get farther away from the river."

The Iroquois pointed south and west. "These lands are crawling with tribes. The council is over. They will all be going home."

"What council?" asked Mahmoud.

"The Iroquois nations. All the tribes. Oskanondonha called it. Oskanondonha -- the Oneida. Everyone knows him. 'Pine Tree.'" He shook his head at Mahmoud's ignorance.

"The Nations voted to quit the British war," said Shooting Star.

"Why?"

"Redcoats keep everything for themselves." He spat.

They could hear sounds rushing water in the distance. *Unity of command.* The phrase registered in Mahmoud's mind like an echo. *General Burgoyne is losing his unity of command.* Master Frestel would be pleased at the idea.

A heron flew clumsily overhead.

"The Lenape will leave us alone. But those Seneca -- " Shooting Star looked at Mahmoud and shook his head ruefully. "We don't want to meet up with them. They don't ask questions."

Mahmoud took another handful of berries.

"Why did Red Wolf tie you up?"

"While all the chieftains were at the Onyota'aka, I gave lessons to two of Red Wolf's women." Shooting Star laughed. "They told me I am better than Red Wolf," (this is not the exact phrasing he used) he bragged.

"I am sick of him getting everything," Shooting Star added, bitterly. It was a sentiment that many young men share.

"I have six friends," he commented. "We may start a new tribe."

They stood up.

"Where do you walk?" asked the Iroquois brave.

"That way. South," answered Mahmoud. "I must find one of the colonial leaders, a friend of mine. And soon. I have important news for him."

"That is good," said Shooting Star. "I go there, too."

"You owe me nothing," said Mahmoud.

"Tah onatut *ahkwa* katiwiki'ik *yahatih*," said Shooting Star, as if this were a response.

He bundled the pouch and stuck it in the knapsack.

"I was going south anyway," he said.

CHAPTER 8
Shooting Star

If these difficulties are not removed,
the consequences will be bad.

-- Sagoyewatha

THE LOCAL COLONIALS HAD TAKEN over Beckman's Mill once the English were driven out by Morgan and his Virginia Raiders. Families had set up stores in one bank of stalls, booths where the women could trade goods and commune.

The mill wheel spun. The buckets rose and fell, spilling the water. The wheel ground the flour. Horses pawed the earth, waiting for the wagons to be filled so they could go on their way.

"Beg your pardon, Ma'am," said the stranger with his hat slouched over his face.

"I am looking for a young man. He is a Persian, with olive skin. He is the son of an old friend. He was wearing a blue jacket. A little gaudy, I'm afraid."

"By what name is he known?" asked the girl.

"He sometimes calls himself Nitidus. His given name is Mahmoud."

"Nitidus was with the Rangers, when we chased the redcoats away," said a woman in the next stall. "My husband calls him a patriot."

"That he is, ma'am. He will be so happy to hear the news from his family. He has a new baby brother. Is he hereabouts?"

"He is not," came the answer. "He set out west and south."

"West to the river. Then south, towards Pennsylvania, I believe. He seeks another."

The stranger thanked her. He bought three pints of milk.

The mill wheel turned with the force of water moving to the sea. Men walked to and fro.

* * *

All winter, snows collect in a vast Adironack watershed, stretching from a mountain once called Cloudsplitter to Calamity Brook to the Opalescent River to Feldpsar Brook. These headwaters gather in Lake Tear of the Clouds. There they begin the descent through shallow flumes and narrow cascades down stone basins. The Seneca call it "River from Beyond the Peaks." Long before the river becomes navigable, the vast canopy of woods spreads itself to the margin of the river, overhanging the water, shadowing its clear blue current.

"We must go higher, and as fast as we can," explained Shooting Star. "Up the mountain. Red Wolf hates to climb.

"He is still following. He will guess where we are going, get there first, and lie in wait for us."

For hours they ran, moving fast over broken land and along crooked ancient footpaths among the trees, avoiding roads. Mahmoud saw nothing but impenetrable walls of foliage, and quickly came to understand that his Iroquois companion had maps in his head, more accurate than any man could draw. They were moving along some kind of meridians, lines of travel from eons past, and modern man could not see them.

The once-Prince of the ottoman Empire gave himself up to the forward motion. They found footholds on sheer sloped and climbed over tracts of giant fallen logs, grabbing onto new growth to steady themselves. They moved rough uncut forest like ghosts, and Mahmoud had no rational understanding of how they were doing it.

He simply followed Shooting Star.

Questions of how and why fell away.

The intricacy of the route allowed them no chance of dialogue.

Mahmoud kept waiting for them to stop. They slowed to a fast trot. Mahmoud had never run so far, for so long.

They traveled in the bed of a shallow brook, leaving no trail.

As a point of pride, Mahmoud tried not to let on how tired he was. His thighs ached, his calves were on fire, and one of his hips seemed about to seize up in cramps. He imitated the loping, easy stride of Shooting Star, who could apparently run all day and all night without slowing.

They jogged downhill in silence, passing vistas of spectacular beauty.

Mahmoud changed the balance of his gait, in imitation of his companion, and was able to keep a decent pace until nightfall.

* * *

"What are you praying to?" asked Shooting Star in the morning. He was seated on the end of a mossy log, at the edge of a stream. The streams were becoming wider and deeper as they neared the Hudson.

"Mecca," answered Mahmoud.

The Iroquois brave was cutting a stiff branch into an arrow he could use to kill Red Moon. He inspected the shaft.

"'Makah.'"

"Mecca."

"Micah." Shooting Star nodded. "It is a heavenly object."

"No. It is a place."

"Ah."

The young Iroquois warrior inserted tail feathers in the tiny slits at the base of the arrow.

"Do you have gods?" asked Shooting Star.

"Aye. One. One god. His name is Allah."

"Al-lach, you say? Ar-lah?"

"Allah. *Allahu akbar. Masha allah.* Thanks be to Allah. *Bismi allah.* In the name of Allah."

"I see," said the Iroquois. "We have gods. They are fierce fighters." He chewed the fish. He made sure Mahmoud's share was larger than his own.

"Allah," said Shooting Star. "Al-lah. Biz-mee Al-lah."

* * *

Near noon of the second morning, they came to a flat meadow filled with an eerie silence. No birds could be seen foraging in the yellow grasses or heard singing, or glimpsed gliding above in the breezes.

It was a battlefield from some massive prehistoric clash. The still-scarred lands held a terrible majesty. No fox or badger moved at their advance. All was still on the dead plain.

As the boys moved through it, they saw bleached bones and skeletons still locked in the embrace of combat. Here and there in the soil were artifacts of war, arrowheads and metal sections of spears, and once or twice they saw what might have been swords.

Here the enemy hosts might have stood, assembled beneath banners in neat lines, listening to their leaders speak of lofty intentions. Here they might have retreated, when the tactics broke down, and a second wave of crude, hand-to-hand battle was fought. Here the last stand might have taken place, where hope and higher purpose had vanished and only death remained.

One might have said it was the Comanche, for they are the most warlike of all, but they have never been known to come this far east. For the savagery of the fighting, you might as well say the Cimbri, or the brutish Barad-Dur, or the mentally unstable Seleucids, yet those tribes all lived and fought a world away from this. Perhaps an expanding Numic empire had met the imperial ambitions of a Prince of the Shoshone.

As they walked through the battlefield. they saw broken remnants of stone arches, giving evidence of where some royal pavilion had stood. They saw heavy rocks next to skulls, marking where woman had walked among the wounded foes with their marrow-cracking mallets to finish it. There were the remains of shallow graves with smaller skeletons, a reminder that even the innocent pay the wages of war.

Here, Mahmoud thought he could make out the rotted wood of two great wheels, lying on their sides. No statue or monument or victory obelisk remained, no stone-sculpted account that might explain why the two hosts had fought and died eons ago, whether it had been land or livestock or water, rivalry in love or race hatred or sheer pride.

Could they still hear the clash of metal and the song of pipes ... or was it just the wind?

* * *

The once-Prince was pleased that he seemed to be able to keep pace with the Indian brave, although he suspected the Iroquois was holding back.

"That jacket you wear is exceedingly ugly," commented Shooting Star.

"You may think so," answered Mahmoud.

"Does all your tribe dress that way?"

"No."

"Good."

They turned around a grove of spruce at the little end of a pond and came to a clearing.

They had been able to avoid all settlements up to now, but this –

A girl, no more than twelve, looked up at them.

She was kneeling in a row of vegetables, in a generous garden. A garden tool was in her hand. She wore a pretty calico dress, blue and white, with an apron in front. Beyond, they could see a log cabin with smoke curling from the chimney, and flowers along its window sills.

Nothing else o the property stirred.

No settlers, no guards. Just the girl.

Shooting Star moved towards her.

She was too frightened to move.

Mahmoud moved to block his friend's path.

Shooting Star turned his gaze from the girl to Mahmoud.

The Iroquois' eyes had changed, and in their flat gaze Mahmoud saw murder – or, more precisely, death, for Shooting Star would only consider it a fair fight for survival, and not murder.

The Ottoman youth gripped the knife in his hand.

At least I will die like a man –

Shooting Star looked at the knife.

Beyond the girl, a dog barked.

Shooting Star glanced in the running dog's direction and adjusted his feet, preparing to gut him.

"*No!*" cried the girl.

Mahmoud shifted his weight, preparing to fight --

Shooting Star looked at Mahmoud's legs, then for a long moment into Mahmoud's eyes.

The once-Prince became overly aware of the tap of a woodpecker somewhere in the leafy woods nearby, a busy creature who knew nothing of right and wrong. Now the tapping was joined by the idiotic call of a jay.

Shooting Star turned on one heel.

The Iroquois youth trotted off, and in the blink of an eye he had entered the high dark arches of the forest and disappeared among the tall, straight trunks of the pines, headed north.

CHAPTER 9

Trap by a Tree

The toils and dangers of the wilderness
were to be encountered before
the adverse hosts could meet.

-- James Fenimore Cooper

IT WAS A GIANT WHITE spruce, over three hundred years old, judging by its growth and girth, and would have looked more at home in one of the swamps that dot the river's estuary, hundreds of miles to the south.

Mahmoud looked out over the expanse of land. The gleaming Hudson River was two miles wide, and he could see the currents swirling. Below him a sharp grassy decline led to a gorge, then a wooded plain and then the river's banks. He would find a canoe and get himself south, towards Gilbert, at twice the speed than he ever could on land.

It is a treasure of a river, he thought. *I can see why the British want it so badly --*

The white spruce sat on a dramatic promontory jutting out over the Hudson Valley. Travelers often stopped under its wind-twisted branches, for it offered one of the most dramatic vistas in all the Hudson Valley.

"Raise your hands, boy," said a deep voice.

The command was repeated in French. "Are you Persian?"

Mahmoud looked up to see a stocky Indian chieftain standing over him, knife drawn.

A white man stood smirking at his side. His rifle was aimed at Mahmoud's heart.

"You! You are the one who freed my prisoner -- "

"Are you Red Wolf?" asked Mahmoud.

"Aye."

"This is the one you were looking for?" asked the white man. "Well, we've got you, Persian, and we'll soon catch your friend, too -- "

"I'll take the jacket." Red Wolf ripped the jacket from Mahmoud. "You won't need it where you're goi -- "

Mahmoud's leg sweep upended Red Wolf.

The white man fired and missed.

A second shot rang out, then a volley of others.

The white man, who had attracted most of the fire, lay sprawled and bleeding -- all but dead -- on the ground.

Red Wolf had vaulted over the ledge and landed in the horseshoe-shaped footpath below. He disappeared among the pines.

Kace the Cossack and Daniel Morgan and three Virginians ran to the ledge and poured bullets into the pines.

"The bastards hide down in the pines, waiting to ambush innocent travelers," said Morgan once the firing had ceased. "We've been hunting them -- "

"Master Kace!" cried Mahmoud. "Is it some miracle, or is it really you?"

"Aye, young Prince," said Kace, "Your family sent me to retrieve you. And I've had the devil finding you -- "

The Rangers dug three bodies from the pines below.

"Red Wolf got away," they called up.

"He took your jacket, too -- " Morgan clapped Mahmoud on the back.

"*Look!*"

One of the Rangers pointed upstream, to where a grouping of boats as big as a flotilla had just rounded the bend. There were dozens of bateaux, muscular with troops and flatbed barges stacked with supplies, and skiffs and shells, all filled with redcoats.

They could see light artillery, wheeled cannons, banners of the British Empire waving in the sunlight.

"It's Burgoyne," said Morgan. "He must have ten thousand men with him.

"We've got to stop him -- "

CHAPTER 10

Downriver

The line of conduct seems now chalked out.
Blows must decide.

-- King George III

"BY THE GODS, YOU'RE THIN – man, you're a right colonial!"

Now Mahmoud wore a buckskin jacket, like the Rangers. He could not stop smiling to see his friend Kace here in the New World, by his side. As empty as he had once felt, now he was filled. With such a companion, he feared nothing.

By the campfire that night, among the canoes they had pulled onto the flat banks of the stream, he told Kace of his adventures. Kace wanted to hear the story of the crossing and the Bosun's Mate twice (he had already heard about the battle at the mill).

"It's more than luck you have around your wrist, and wrapped all around you. You should have died three times already, from what you tell me."

They had found a tributary stream to the Hudson, one that ran parallel to it. The redcoat flotilla had stopped for the night a mile upriver, or so Morgan's scouts reported.

"We must have dropped a hundred feet in less than a mile," judged Kace.

He consulted the map, then his compass, then the map again.

"This is a fine land," said Kace. "Worth fighting for."

"The Colonials may well lose," said Mahmoud. "A third of them are with the British. And the British know how to fight a war."

"Then their sons will still be fighting, years hence," said Kace. "Never have I seen folk so determined."

The once-Prince traced a line on the map.

"This corridor -- " said Mahmoud. He pointed to the eastern Great Lakes, Champlain and Ontario, then traced the Hudson river down as it bisected Lake George, then the Mohawk and Pioneer Valleys. "It is a mirror image of the Battle of Rashidun. Burgoyne has studied it. 'Control the waterway, control the supplies.'

"Gage comes in from Trenton, that's what Morgan thinks.

"They intend to catch Washington in a pincer," continued Mahmoud, late of the Selestat School for Young Monarchs at *Nid de Corbeau.* "As sure as we breathe. Look at the direction. They're not fighting, they're positioning." He looked at his companion. "The colonials' only chance is if we interrupt the communications between Howe and Burgoyne. They must not be allowed to coordinate."

"Let us deliver the letter and be gone," concluded Kace. "We have too many enemies here."

* * *

"I've been thinking," said Kace the next evening.

"If what you said is true – if you are disinherited -- then we should set up shop here. In America. You and me.

"Think of it. We could set up a boat-works along this river, or in Boston. The colonials appreciate good work, and boats will run, war or no war.

"We could buy land," he added. "There is room for everyone in America."

"But our people need to hear these ideas," said Mahmoud, although he had not thought about it before. "We should tell them how a republic of free men can work. They would love that on the Bosporus."

Kace took the pipe from his mouth and whistled. He leaned back and looked up at the night sky.

As Perseus and Aries and Taurus twinkled above him in the great machines of night, Mahmoud felt that he belonged. There, in the New World, under the patterned stars, he was earning a place in the world, and friends who loved him.

By the fire, Kace told old stories from Cossack prehistory, stories of the Rurikid Princes and Yaroslav the Wise, stories of his people which were mostly boring until he got to Kyivan Rus and the Ruin, and the endlessly violent protections of the Hetmanate, until Mahmoud fell asleep.

CHAPTER 11

The Battle by the Creek

War is not what you think it is.

-- John Nagl

THE SADIST APPLIED THE POISON as he held the bayonet blade low over the fire.

Major Alexander Lindsay, Sixth Earl of Balcarres, villain of Bunker Hill, a tall, elegant man, prepared for battle.

It was before dawn yet. Battle was coming; these woods were teeming with Colonials.

Carelessly, Balcarres stood in the clearing, over the fire. He was painting poison on the bayonets of his five rifles. He had learned the poison from the Cayuga: snake venom mixed with certain dark-colored roots.

"They'll be dead the moment this breaks the skin," he chuckled. Few of his lieutenants were in hearing range.

"Dead but still on their feet," he mused. "Stupid farmers ..."

His own men recoiled from Balcarres, for all fair-thinking soldiers shun such things as poisons.

"Hah! That's better," said Balcarres to the liquid drying on the blade. It had been too runny on the first round, and would not adhere to the blade, so he had thickened the liquid poison with powdered bark until it was a paste.

"Oh, the Continentals will feel your sting," he said, with relish bordering on glee --

The first bullet struck Balcarres in the shoulder, spinning him around. He did not know it, but Balcarres was felled by a rotating bullet, one shot from a grooved barrel, a rare round which came far and level and true.

The second bullet penetrated his skull at the base, killing him.

The third bullet waited until he lay on the leafy ground, and struck him unceremoniously in the stomach, causing his corpse to jerk.

A rock was lobbed into the clearing. One of the British lieutenants saw that a note was attached.

He carefully removed the note and smoothed it out. It read as follows:

That was payback for what Balcarres did at Bunker Hill. A Just Kill.

The handwriting was uncommonly neat. By the graceful curves and the handsome proportions of the letters, they could tell that the writer was a man of intelligence and compassion.

Below the main message was this postscript:

The rest of you should leave now.

It was signed "Daniel Morgan," but did not look like the composition of a backwoodsman.

* * *

"All right gentlemen," said Horatio Gates, a straightforward fellow with no airs. "How do we propose to win this?"

"Ask him," said Morgan, nodding his head at Mahmoud. "He knows a thing or two."

Gates turned to Mahmoud.

"The English say there are nine rules of war. You are currently breaking four of them." Mahmoud looked up at Gates for emphasis. "You can't win."

"And what might you suggest?" asked Gates.

"Well, sir," said Mahmoud, "Burgoyne's Indians have quit him, so -- "

"The Iroquois!" asked Gates keenly. "Quit him! Are you sure, son?"

"Yes sir. I encountered a brave who had participated in the War Council. *Onyota'aka* he called it. He said Oskanondonha had summoned them for a vote. And they voted to stay out of the white man's fray.

"Without the Six Nations, I would estimate that Burgoyne brings twelve thousand men down from Bennington with him. The Hessians will follow, they are slow of foot and always a day behind. It is a small auxiliary force – no more than two hundred – but they are accurate.

"With a host that size, Burgoyne is trained to establish and secure his supply lines, wait for his full force to gather, and advance on the enemy in three columns. Yet he is pinned to the river. If we can construct enough fortifications on the flood plain, and with our cannons on the heights, we can dominate all his movements. They need to haul all of their supplies up from the river – men, horses, munitions, food. We can frustrate that effort."

"Interrupt their supply lines," nodded Morgan.

"Yes. *'Place the enemy in a position of disadvantage through the flexible application of combat power.'* The seventh rule of war," said Mahmoud.

"Seventh rule, eh?" laughed Gates.

"Very well. Take the New Yorkers. They have two regiments."

"But how do we build such fortifications?" asked a young officer.

"The engineer. Kosciusko," said Kace. "He will know."

They called for the Polish engineer, and he eagerly drew out a scheme and supervised (with Kace to interpret for him) the realization of it. Fifty of Israel Putnam's men joined in the ambitious job, and by that evening a system of redoubts, trenches, and battlements were in place. A cadre of Vermonters fashioned a crude abatis, and then a row of fascines – great bundles of sticks bound together. The Virginians sank caissons along the swamp's edge.

The next morning, nervous colonials across the heights watched the British carefully.

So ingenious were Kosciusko's designs and so sound their construction that the British could scarcely move, let alone unpack and deploy their munitions. Twice the engineer sought to run down and improve some feature of his work, and twice Kace restrained him.

With the colonial fortifications frustrating their expanse, the British were entirely dependent on the riverbed. They could only proceed downstream and emerge where the colonials wanted them to, in the open meadows of the farmer's lower fields, where the rebel positions awaited them.

"Very well," said Gates. "Now we see what Johnny decides. Let's dispatch Ebenezer's brigade (by which he meant the 2nd, 8th and 9th Massachusetts) here," he pointed to his map, "and Ten Broeck behind him. First, Second and Third New Hampshire are here, along the lower banks. Let them retreat to Saratoga if they like, but nowhere else."

"Bring word to Arnold," he told a young officer, "that he is to hold his position. Absolutely nothing offensive. Not until he hears from me." He scribbled a note. "He won't like that," Gates added as the officer mounted his horse.

"Sir," said Mahmoud. "You need an expeditionary force. We must know all of Burgoyne's movements, not just what we see from here --"

"Scouts," said Morgan. "We'll do it."

All agreed that Mahmoud, with his letters for Lafayette, should remain a spectator and advisor, to protect his true value to the colonial cause. Kace stayed at his side.

* * *

"The boy was right," said Morgan at noon, when he had returned from his scouting. "Gentleman Johnny is all bottled up. See him casting to and fro. See that one officer, in front there, moving so quick and smart? Cadmon tells me that is Simon Fraser. He is the one our boys should take out of the battle, if God wills it. Hup, here they go now ..."

They could see scurries of movement among the masses of redcoats. Horses were being urged into action, wagons were being turned --

"He's headed west. Trying to bust through our flank."

"He's headed towards Freeman's place."

A small clutch of colonials, led by a tall, blond, red-faced young officer, approached them up the slope. It was General Arnold.

"Sir, they will attempt a second flanking maneuver, as sure as day. I saw it at Hubbardton."

"We have Morgan and the Rangers scouting across the western banks, up to the loyalist's farms," answered Gates coldly. "And what we face bears little resemblance to Hubbardton. That was a morning's siege and two dozen volleys."

"I request permission to take the 31st regiment down into the flood plain," said Arnold. "I mean to test Burgoyne."

"Permission denied," said Gates testily, turning to face Arnold directly. "Stop second-guessing me or you will soon surrender your command, sir.

"Dearborn, you and your men take the left flank. Stay along the ridge. Mark the enemy movements and send me word what you see. Kill any British officers as you may," he added.

"You may return to your positions, General," Gates commanded Arnold, choosing to further humiliate the junior officer. "We must hold the Heights, at all costs. It is vital to our plan. We all must play ours part, un-heroic as they may seem at the time."

* * *

Crisp detonations told that Burgoyne hoped to use his cannons from the decks of his barges. That would not work well, even if it were German artillery.

Burgoyne threw a corps of Germans forward on the east side of the lake to seize the road there. But the road was swampy and the Germans, expecting fair passage, slowed to a halt. These roads were not capable of transporting the artillery they so treasured. The colonials, who cared not whether the terrain was swamp or snow or lava from a volcano, advanced and seized the roads.

From their perch at the farmhouse, up the slope, Mahmoud and his Cossack companion watched as this first arm of the redcoats advanced up the hill and met with the rebels' impediments and strong fences. The British attack was altogether formal, two ranks moving on a front almost half-a-mile long toward the set battle line, a line formed by the stone walls along Freeman's Farm on one side, and the colonial barricades on the other. The British were hurt by musket fire. Howe sent word to Burgoyne by a boat, and directed the fleet to set fire to Charlestown. The river battery threw a parcel of shells, which landed with a show of flames and smoke. Then came the slow forward movement of the main battle line: two ranks of scarlet-clad grenadiers and light infantrymen, almost 2,000 in all, marching in full kit, each man carrying pounds of knapsacks, blankets, food, and ammunition -- across irregular fields of knee-deep grass. The American troops—no more than 1, 500 men at any time, at the end only half that—held their fire until the first British line was within 150 feet of the barricades; when they fired, it was almost at point-blank range, and the result was slaughter.

The British front line collapsed in heaps of dead and wounded -- "as thick as sheep in a field." Great gaps appeared in the once parade-perfect ranks, and the survivors spun back. Hessians ascended the hill directly into the rebel entrenchments. To the left the enemy poured in fresh troops over the land. Hills round the country were covered with spectators. "The storm of the redoubts ... filled the eye," wrote one later, "and the reflection that perhaps a defeat was a final loss to the British empire in America filled the mind."

The British regrouped for a second attack, directed now squarely at the redoubt and breastwork. The Americans withheld fire until the last moment, and when it came it tore the line of upright marching redcoats to shreds: "an incessant stream of fire poured from the rebel lines," as a British officer described it. The forward units fell back against the second line moving up, then turned and fled back down the hill. Burgoyne called for a third assault, a bayonet charge against the central barricades. As the third charge neared the line of fortification, the rebels' powder ran out. They

could not sustain their fire. Grenadiers and light infantrymen poured over the parapets and through the thin barricades, and dove into groups of colonial defenders.

* * *

The wounded were carried to the porch of the farmhouse, which was being used as a field hospital. Kace and Mahmet helped with dressings and medicines as best they could.

The front door swung open and Arnold appeared. Frustrated with his orders to defend and not attack, he had been drinking, and was swaying slightly. Powerful emotions gripped him.

"We must SEIZE the MOMENT, my boys! Burgoyne is hurt – if we attack now, we can deal him a fatal blow." Arnold, who was well-liked, was slurring his words, and this gave his listeners pause.

"He's right," announced Mahmoud. He stood up. "I'm in!"

"You're not," said Kace, pulling the Prince back.

But in the confusion of Arnold and a shouting wave of his loud, loyal men rushing to join the fight, Mahmoud escaped.

Kace could not find him.

The next phase of the battle cost Burgoyne nearly 400 men, including the capture of most of the grenadiers' command, and six of the ten field pieces brought to the action. Morgan's snipers felled Simon Fraser, and Burgoyne himself was also very nearly killed by one of Morgan's marksmen; three shots hit his horse, hat and waistcoat.

Mahmoud fought in the center of the fray, side by side with Ten Broeck and his militia brigade. He fired carefully, accurately, aiming to wound and not to kill.

Just as the militia men clashed directly with the Hessians regiment, six Iroquois braves joined the melee, entering from the woods to the North.

They quickly gravitated to where young Mahmoud stood firing and surrounded him.

He was too busy to see that it was his friend Shooting Star making good on his debt. The Iroquois protected him as though he were Hannibal at Ipres, and let no redcoat near.

As so often happens in battle, this most excellent intent had a contrary effect: the Hessians and professional soldiers, seeing the Iroquois so fiercely guard the Ottoman boy, decided that he must be critical to the colonial cause. To repay the colonials for shooting Fraser, they focused all their fire upon Mahmoud.

Standing bravely in a deadly hail of bullets, the once-Prince rallied the colonials.

Then, in the space of a minute, everything critical happened almost at once.

Kace, locating his friend at last, ran to join him.

Red Wolf – wearing the jacket he had stolen from Mahmoud – appeared from the British ranks and screamed at the once-Prince of the Ottomans, even as he leapt to kill him.

Shooting Star jumped between them and saved Mahmoud.

Mahmoud was struck down with the flat of Red Wolf's tomahawk.

Shooting Star was felled by a British bullet.

Red Wolf rose to apply the coup de grace to the young Ottoman --

As he ran, Kace saw a lone figure on the eastern cliffs. He looked out of place. Kace realized the man's rifle was a Turkish hunting rifle, with an inlaid wood stock that glinted in the sunlight. The figure aimed his rifle directly at Mahmoud --

"*No*" cried Kace, but he was too late. The assassin fired.

The figure who fell was not Mahmoud but Red Wolf. The assassin had seen the jacket, not realizing it was not the Prince who wore it.

Kace fired twice and the assassin fell, toppling off the cliff.

Three British rounds struck Mahmoud.

* * *

"The wound is deep," said Kace. "Are you in pain?"

"Yes," said Mahmoud. "I do not care for it."

All around him was the cascading firing and rush of soldiers on the battlefield. The Colonials gambled and rushed forward, hoping to gain the high ground.

"Oh! I am not even seventeen! How can this be -- "

Kace fumbled to staunch the wound. He wrapped his own shirt all the way around the boy's chest; it was no use. The shirt reddened, soaked.

"I am a fool," said Mahmoud as he looked into the face of his old friend.

"No fool, lad. You have lived a lifetime in these past months. Why, you may have single-handedly saved the Colonial side!"

Mahmoud choked on blood. He coughed, and his voice grew weak.

"I have not fulfilled the pact -- "

"I will give the papers to your friend, Gilbert," said Kace. "I will find him. I swear it."

"How lucky I was to meet you," said Mahmoud to the older man. He tried to place his hand on Kace's arm, but it fell short.

"The luck is all mine, my Prince." The big man leaned close, so those fading eyes could see him, and hear his voice.

Mahmoud spat blood.

"Let go," said Kace." You can let go now."

"Oh! Oh!" Mahmoud squeezed the Cossack's hand. "I see my home -- "

"I will carry you there, son. You will sleep in the next life close by your kin -- "

The third and most capable son of the Sabdulhamid, Sultan of All the Ottoman Lands, gave a last gurgle.

Life left his frame.

Kace closed Mahmoud's eyes.

The tall, burly Cossack moved slowly, sadly as he carried the body.

All rifle fire on the battlefield at Saratoga paused, until he had passed.

CHAPTER 12

A Letter Arrives (Once More)

Occasionally - oh, very rarely! - the cogs fit.

-- Robert E. Howard

"*Are these the men with* which I am to defend America?" asked George Washington.

He stood at the window. He meant the soldiers who marched in ragged lines in the field beyond.

"Are they? *Hmmm?*"

He said it with such genuine distress, with such personal pain, like someone who had just been told he had contracted a disease, that the page felt he had to respond.

"Why, yes sir," answered the page, who had only come into the General's office to announce the presence of a visitor. "Those are the men of the Thirty-first brig --"

"Is the WILL OF GOD?" shouted Washington. "By the LIVING CHRIST, is this to be my fate?"

"W-w-well, s-s-sire, I know not -- " stammered the page.

"*Will you shut up!*" Washington cuffed the boy. "What could you possibly kn-- "

The visitor burst through the entrance. The burly Cossack seized Washington by the lapels and jammed him against the wall.

"*Take some care with the common soldier, Gen'rl,*" Kace snarled. "He does his share."

Washington, unused to such rough treatment, sputtered and flailed, but not until the young French officer intervened did Kace release the General.

"Are ye Gilbert Motier, Marquis de Lafayette?" Kace asked the young Frenchman.

"I am," said Gilbert.

"I come here to represent Prince Mahmoud, of the Ottomans."

Washington fought back. Kace renewed his grip on the larger man. The General's eyes widened --

"Stop! Stop!" exclaimed Gilbert.

He dissuaded the Cossack from strangling Washington.

"Do you speak of my school-mate, son of the Sitting Sultan of Constantinople, Prince of Topkapi? Nitidus? What news? Tell me, friend. I am eager to know of his safe passage and his whereabouts."

"I come from Saratoga," said Kace.

"Mahmet gave his life to save mine in that battle.

"You will meet no man so fine or so brave, such as that boy.

"His last request was that I bring these documents …"

Kace reached into the furs which adorned his bulk and produced four letters.

"To deliver to you."

PART TWO

Members of the Pact

In a revolution, as in a novel,
the most difficult part to invent is the end.

-- Alexis de Tocqueville

CHAPTER 13
Louis XVI

Bombs bursting in the ballrooms of Versailles
would not have surprised the foggy-eyed ministers
in Louis XVI's court more than
the American victory at Saratoga.

-- French Newspaper account of the Battle of Saratoga

"YOU COME WITH LETTERS?" THE King asked his visitor from America. "From Lafayette?"

Ben Franklin, the Colonials' ambassador to the Court of Louis XVI, nodded. This time, he did not bow.

"Perhaps this will move our joint efforts along," said the minister testily.

"Nothing moves unless it is pushed," said Franklin. "You asked for solid proof of the strength of the revolution before he would officially commit French military aid to the cause.

"We gave you Saratoga.

"You asked for terms. You will find these terms more than favorable. They are extraordinary."

"The work of the Marquis de Lafayette -- " sniffed the Minister.

"And his young friends," said Franklin.

"Show us the letters and we can consider your request," said the Minister.

"This is no longer a request," replied Franklin. "This is an offer. If you decline, or

if you hesitate, my next stop is the Spanish embassy. At my discretion, these terms can be transferred directly to other parties."

The first letter was this:

In all Sectors of the Ocean Seas, Russia directs its own operatives as well as its varied licensed fleets of privateers that, as of the above date, the American flag is to be honored.

Great Britain is a declared foe.

Through the agency Mickler Sykes of Amsterdam, we hereby declare a regulation for all Russian vessels to sub-contract exclusively with French merchant vessels for transport, supplies, and repair. In addition, French ships are to be granted rights-of-way in the following ports and districts: Adriatic, Arctic, and Azov Seas; the shipyards of Sebastopol; Baltic, Bering and Barents Seas; the Imperial fleet's docks at Kherson; the Don Flotilla; the Mediterranean ports of Cerigo, Zante, Kefalonia; and the Santa Maura islands.

These terms apply so long as the Nation of France is an active war partner to the Colonial Americans, who stand for the rights and privileges of the common man. We find England's opposition to a free American colony abhorrent.

We extend these terms in solidarity with our brethren in the American Colonies.

Signed,

Fyodor Ushakov
Admiral of the Baltic Fleet, Sovereign Republic of Russia

Counter-signed

Catherine Ekatarina Alexeenva
Catherine the Great
Signed this 8th day of November, 1776

And the red wax seal of the House of Romanov adorned it, on the bottom right.

The second letter was written on the letterhead of the shipping agency Mickler, Sykes Satterthwaite and Jaap of Amsterdam (with offices in Oslo, St. Petersburg, Johannesberg, Hong Kong and Cirebon)

Letter of Credit

On behalf of our client, the Oldenbarnveldt Family Holdings LLC, and in specific appreciation of the efforts of France to aid the colonial cause in America, we offer a line of credit along these terms: two million gilders rising to ten million, on a rotating basis, at an interest of four per cent annually.

The funds are liquid as of the above date, and remain available to the Crown of France so long as they support and defend the American Colonial military forces as delineated by their ambassador, Benjamin Franklin of Philadelphia, in writing (attached). Interest payments are due on the first of each month. The entire principal is due twenty-four months after the end date as noted above.

Signed,

Johannes Mickler
Johannes Mickler
Pietr Oldenbarneveldt, Director VOC

The letter's postscript went on to assign the Bank of the Netherlands as the lead bank.

The third letter was decorated with an elaborate border of celestial symbols and a crimson Islamic seal. It read as follows:

In accordance with the Law of the Sea as determined in the recent Treaty of Kocuk Kaynarca, and with respect to all its maritime territories in 32 provinces and numerous vassal states, the Ottoman Suzereignty commands that the French Republic of Louis XVI, Absolute Monarch of France and Navarre, receive right of innocent passage and peaceful transit wheresoever French vessels seek it.

Furthermore, it is declared from this date that we remove legal protection from all privateers, buccaneers, pirates, or independent captains who interfere with France's said right, in all the above areas of jurisdiction.

Lastly, fishing rights in the above jurisdictions are to be granted to any and all vessels sailing under French colors.

This document is predicated on and limited to the expanse of time in which the Throne is in Active Alliance with the North American Colonials in their righteous battle for human freedom against the Tyrant King George III.

The maritime shipping agency Mickler, Sykes and Satterthwaite is this document's sole arbiter.

Solemnly sworn this 6th Day of December, 1776,
Kemal Deviet i -Aliyye i - Osmaniyye
Admiral of the Royal Ocean Fleet, Knight of the Permanent Order of Seraphim
Minister of Maritime Affairs of the Ottoman Sultanate

The fourth was from Lafayette himself, and regarded an extraordinary grant of access to South China Sea lanes and the entirety of the Emperor's Grand Canal. It would be beyond value to a young American nation. This note, the Minister read silently. Then he whispered its contents to Louis.

"How extraordinary," said Louis XVI when he had heard all three documents read aloud. He made no motion to quit his train-making.

"And timely," added Franklin. "The moths in your empty coffers are lonely."

"Just a moment -- " said the Finance Minister indignantly.

"*Who are you to* -- " said Louis.

"I am an American Colonial," said Franklin, all etiquette having left his voice, his manner suddenly fiercely honest, "and lives have been sacrificed so that I could bring you these letters."

Louis, no stranger to strong and fast-changing emotions, glanced at his advisor.

"Henri?"

"It is a set of most useful offers," said the Minister of Finance. "Useful to glory of France."

"Very well. You have a document for me to sign, Colonial?"

Franklin offered it. The King took a pen from his desk and signed it, with a flourish.

So France entered the American Revolution, on the side of the colonials, opposing Britain.

CHAPTER 14
Will Receives Two Visitors

The pain I feel now is the happiness
I had before. That's the deal.

-- C.S. Lewis

AMSTERDAM, AUGUST 1775

"Willow?"

The crowded floor of the shipping agency was a panorama of movement and commerce, sights and sounds and exotic smells. Men wheeled barrows and crates among the long tables, checking off lists and calling instructions, pointing to booths and stalls and portals leading to piers of store-rooms and adjacent wharfs.

"Willow?" asked the visitor.

In an adjacent open room sat a team of seated scribes, copying certain documents at their long tables among neat reams of paper and bottles of ink, hot wax and seals in their holders, colored maps and contracts, flat pouches waiting for couriers to deliver word to Dubin, in Selestat, to Alexandria, to both Capes, to Yoruba, to Tientsin, to Mordwywr (the Cornwall coast, that is). To Cynthiana, in Constantinople.

Will Oldenbarneveldt was seated in a quiet back room, a cubbyhole in a berth off the agency's main floor. One of the wharf cats sat on his lap..

The stranger stood in the doorway of the trading-floor back office.

"Are you Will O?" he asked. "Will Oldenbarnevelt?"

The gangly youth was too well-dressed to be a messenger, too skinny to be a seaman.

"I am a notary. With the VOC. Bills of lading and exchange, mostly. I have come up from the Rotterdam office.

"A month ago. I came across the ledgers for a Norwegian expedition to the Chesapeake in which the capital arranger, agent and trustee were all the same party.

"A syndicate of investors led by the Azimuth Corporation.

"Which is you, I believe. Young sir."

Will looked up from his notations.

The cat, displeased by all this talk and interruption, made a show of stretching all four legs. She then re-seated herself on the stool next to Will.

"This is sophisticated structured financing, leveraging any single share or group of shares with a syndicated interest in twelve other cargos," continued the stranger.

"Most innovative. It reduces the risk of any single investor to more-than-acceptable proportions."

The cat glared at the stranger for this ongoing disruption.

"I found expeditions of the Japanese Shogunate to New Holland similarly funded. Then the structure was repeated with the Ottomans, the Muslim *Hituese*, the Bengal *Subah*, always in support of American merchants -- "

"Is there a point to all this?" asked Will.

"Yes. Yes, of course," replied the Notary.

"My first point is that, taken together, this ... this network represents a staggering amount of capital. You have quadrupled the finances of the Colonial rebels. You have set into motion a fleet of transoceanic agents the size of a small navy.

"My second point is that I have left the employ of the VOC.

"In hopes of working with you.

"I ask no salary, not for the first month anyway. I am devoted to the Colonial cause."

A commotion arose on the trading floor, high spirits and loud discussion.

"And what is your name?" asked Will O.

"Joost," answered the Notary. "Joost Satterthwaite."

"Well, Joost Satterthwaite," said Will, moving a stack of documents.

"You'd better pull up a stool.

"*The Northern Queen* departs at eight bells. Her sponsors need articles of lading for thirty palettes of Finnish sardines..."

"Excellent!"

The happy young Notary took his place at the desk beside Will's.

The cat leapt from the stool to the small sofa beneath the curved windows. There, she tested the cushions in regal fashion, letting the room know that it had been her decision to change places.

Tucking her legs under her, the cat blinked twice, a signal that all activities could now continue as before.

* * *

"Oh, Will," called Johannes Mickler.

It was a quiet, un-demanding call, almost a question.

Will Oldenbarnevelt had grown since the day when he fought off a stampeded of pigs in a pen in the hills of Alsace. His frame was taller, sturdier, more filled out, and his long hair fell over the white collar, like Gilbert's.

"We can't interrupt," said Johannes told his companion. "Not just yet. He's preparing to enter a final ledger..."

Deep in thought, Will carefully erased figures and then copied them   until they were just as he wanted them. He dipped his pen in the inkwell, three times, tapping off the excess ink. He bent to memorialize the figures in the ledger; soon they would be permanent records.

In the quiet, they could hear Will humming to himself. It was a folk song, one of these Slavic songs, the songs about seasons ...

"Will. Will my boy," said Johannes Mickler. "You have a visitor. An old friend has come to see you."

His procedures complete, Will looked up.

It was the petite servant girl, the Ovando house-girl. She stood framed in the doorway, a figure of blond curls and light blue patterned dress amid the drab browns and grays and sea- greens of the maritime offices. Her perfume recalled moonlit nights in the forests of *Nid de Corbeau.*

"I told her of our many efforts to locate her after the Ovando estate collapsed," continued Johannes, who seemed most pleased.

"She was on her way to Hungary.

"She has asked to see you -- "

She, too, had grown.

CHAPTER 15
A Duel in Brandenburg

If you lived in any of the lesser German states
at this time, you were fending for yourself.
The Holy Roman Empire was crumbling,
and a united Germany was a century away.

-- A Brief History of Botany

LEO WAVED FROM THE PUNT.

The villagers cheered, cautiously.

The river seemed to preen and gush as its waters rolled through the Brandenburg precincts.

When Mahmoud found the papers of the engineer Riquet, they were able to convince Umukoru and Dubin that extending the old aqueducts spanning the Arzviller Incline

would be relatively easy. Only two new blocks were required to shore up the foundation, and no gates meant no woodwork (which for the Canal, had taken up far more time than masonry). The new waters from this aqueduct would revive the Vosges, the river that ran through Leo's Barony. Restoring the Vosges meant a return of trade with Alsace to the south, and Roshei and Colmar and Riquewihr to the north.

Leo's arrival at sunset, in the pencil boats, floating though the

village square, the revived river's banks decorated with lanterns and ribbons and banners, captured the Barony's attention.

* * *

"Look," said Leo to the room full of angry freeholders.

Faces stared back at him. The people of Thedinghaus had been invited into Castle Ehrbhof to hear him. They were waiting for him to begin.

Leo Krummensee-Grabmaler, Heir to the House of Hohenzollern, Lesser Magistrate of the Margraviate of Brandenburg, stood to address the restless crowd.

Leo stood at a great table on the second floor of his family's castle, the Schloss Erbhof. It was a smallish castle, and in ill repair. One of the grand staircases had been walled off.

Rosemary had put out refreshments. A young man, a visitor, sat politely at one end of the table. On side tables, Leo had set an array of trunks, chests, boxes and maps.

The villagers were uneasy. They were only there because Werner had shown them the Chinese rhubarbs.

"Well! Thank you all. For coming, that is. I – *ah*, I -- " stuttered Leo.

Leo had arrived home, in the boats, on the renewed Vosges river channel. the evening before. Werner and his little girl sat up with Leo's sister, Rosemary – Romy. Leo had showed them the Chinese rhubarb plants and the chest of seeds which would spawn acres more. Werner, deeply impressed, had shown them around the three villages.

"You have all seen the Vosges channel restored. On the way here, this morning, did anyone pass the Dahme?" The once-vigorous stream had been shrunken by a series of dams which the neighboring Prussian estate had built.

"Yes," said one woman. "I did. The river was full, to its banks. I wondered why-- "

"I have spent the season at Selestat, helping build the canal that has opened these waters, too," said Leo. "We added an aqueduct, to carry volume to the Vosges and the Dahme. Now, we can reach all the markets north and east with our goods. And narrow boats to carry them anywhere between Bremen and Alsace.

"I met with Herr Lombard on my way home," he continued. This had been Will's idea, Will and Shay. "It seems that he only wanted a lake so he could go fishing with his grandchildren. I took him to our cabins, on the Nieplitz, on the northern border, where the carp jump into your boat. He now prefers that.

"Herr Lombard has agreed to let the entire Dahme flow free," continued Leo. "We will have full access to those waters. And I believe we can also divert part of the Nieplitz' flow, below the lakes. Here is how I thought we could irrigate -- "

He unrolled the maps Mei Ying had drawn and spread them on the table.

The men and women of the Margrave crowded around. They saw unfolding drawings of extensive gardens with overhead irrigation, ironworks with common forges, a school, an open fencing system, new wells to be dug, and an armory. Murmurs of approval rose as they sifted through drawing after drawing.

"Good," said Leo. "I was nervous. I wasn't sure you would like them.

"I wanted to also show you *this* --"

He rolled out a new map at the table's other end.

"The road to Bremen has been completed," he explained. "From Bremen to Havel." He showed a newspaper announcing as much.

"Havel? That is just over the hill," said a farmer.

"Yes," said Leo. "If we can complete that short stretch, we'll have a path to bring your goods to the Baltic ports. The Baltic markets, I should say.

"But none of the Swedes," said an older freeman, meaning all the Scandinavian traders, "know us. Why would they buy from us?"

Leo removed a letter from the pile.

"I have a copy of a contract," he said. "It is from a shipping agency in Amsterdam, and it states how much wool they are willing to take and at what prices." This, of course, was Will's work.

This announcement caused a stir, and there was shoving and shouting until Werner read the contract aloud.

"It ends with a list of bankers who will advance, to any certified vendor, moneys upon these signed contracts," he concluded. Rosemary displayed a pile of applications, along with the seal she would use to certify them.

"I have pledged my shares in the Margravate against the advance," said Leo. He repeated the statement.

"Your word is your bond. If you cheat me, I will go bankrupt. And we all get nothing."

"Lastly," called Leo. "Lastly," he repeated, and at this point Leo held up his two arms and swiveled them for silence, as he had seen master Dubin do.

"Lastly, I would like you to meet a young man who has come all the way from Leiden. He is a student in medicine, at the university. His name is Ivo Emerich." Gilbert had arranged this introduction, through his grandmother.

Emerich stepped to the table.

"When I read of your symptoms," said the medical student, "I recognized the syndrome. It is not the plague. Professor Boerhaave and I believe you have encountered a variant of a Spanish influenza. Probably one of the imported steers is a carrier."

Emerich swung a small, heavy crate onto the table and opened it, removing bottles of a clear liquid.

"With quinine and alcohol and some thorough scrubbing of your kitchens, I believe we can eliminate the threat. I have brought some star anise and badiam, just in case."

The excitement was such that it was almost an hour before Leo could show his freehold neighbors his (well, Mahmoud's, actually) scheme for constructing way stations along the road to Bremen, as they transported their goods to market.

* * *

The Peenemude library was quiet – silent, or so it seemed to Leo -- as Leo explained the latest turn of events to his cousin and the family Chamberlain, Herr Melton.

Lucien Peenumude had been pleased to see his cousin Leo, at first.

Yet he had grown quiet as the conversation progressed, and when Leo lay the envelope from the banker down on the table, Lucien stiffened.

"You throw the money I lent you back in my face-- " spat Luc.

"With interest-- " corrected Leo.

Herr Melton read the bank document, He nodded to his client. In the long silence that followed, Leo could hear muffled sounds of pleasant conversation and music, perhaps from the ballroom.

Leo had requested that only Luc and his chamberlain, Melton, be present.

He came to the second topic: there would be no wedding to Rosemary. She loved Werner, and would marry him.

"I have consulted an attorney who seems to know about such things," said Leo. He opened a second envelope and slid that letter across the table. Herr Melton read the document.

Lucien's face twisted into a mask of fury.

"Look, I'm no good at this," confessed Leo. "I am trying to show you the utmost respect, Lucien-- "

"You are a *clod*, adding *insult*-- " said Luc angrily.

"And now you *cancel* the wedding between our two houses. It is quite a hero's return-- "

"She doesn't love you." stated Leo. "Tell the courtesan crowd anything you want. There's your money. No longer contact Romy."

Leo turned to leave.

Luc slapped him across the face.

"You don't mean that," said Leo.

"I demand a duel, *armleuchter!*"

Leo was no longer trying to be accommodating.

"You *don't* want that," he warned.

Lucien strode to the double doors and swept the doors open –

"I challenge you to a duel! *Trantute!*" he announced in front of the surprised courtesans of the House of Peenemude.

"A *proper* duel," he added. "You *proper* coward."

"Tomorrow. Dawn," said Leo evenly.

To the chamberlain, Melton, he said, as he left,

"Come early. Bring two sets of pistols, so I may inspect them beforehand."

"I demand a duel, *armleuchter!*" Leo was no longer trying to be accommodating. "You *don't* want that," he warned.

* * *

It begins when the light changes.

It begins when the first light of dawn touches those high branches, where the big-eyed birds see that another day is coming, and jump to defend their territory, and croon to their mates, and generally announce their presence in the world. As the sound and light and morning breezes filter down the crowns of the trees, the uncouth jays, the robins and thrushes join in. Once the steady drum of woodpeckers strikes up, it does not stop. Eventually, all the warbling and all the chiff-chaff – the squirrels and chipmunks, and grasshoppers in the dewy grass, and frogs in the babbling brooks – chime in, and the morning chorus of the ancient forests of Germany rises to greet the traveler.

A dozen witnesses made their slow way through the forest mist to see the duel.

While outlawed, duels attracted a crowd.

Werner and Leo inspected the pistols, taking each from the wooden case.

Herr Melton spoke with each of the duelists.

First Leo and then Lucien took up their pistols and stood back to back.

Herr Melton counted backwards from ten.

They fired at sequential moments, Lucien first and Leo right after; but Lucien's hand bucked wildly with the recoil, and his shot struck a tree ten yards east of his target.

Lucien relaxed, thinking he had been untouched.

Seeing that his own shot had missed, he reached for a second gun, one he had hidden in his vest. Herr Melton leapt to dissuade him from such a dishonorable act--

Then a look of curiosity crossed Luc's features, as if he were hearing or feeling something no one else could hear or feel.

He took a step and staggered, falling to his one knee.

Luc put one hand to his heart.

He reached out the other hand to Leo, as though for a helping hand, forgetting they were enemies today.

Lucien Peenemude looked down and saw blood pouring from his chest.

He fell, never to rise again.

* * *

"It's for the best, *engel--*" said Leo to Romy, who could not stop crying.

"I am happy! Can you not see that?"

The little party accompanying Leo rushed to the trailhead behind Erbhof Castle. The trail would lead him through the forest, to the juncture west of Thedinghaus, where a wagon waited to take him to Bremen and a certain ship bound for Boston.

"But what will you do in America?" asked Romy.

"Fight for the colonial cause," he replied. "My friends are there."

He held her hand as they moved along the path. "I have broken the law. I would only be a burden if I stayed, Sister --"

"Will you return?"

"Of course! I will be the uncle who spoils his nephews and nieces --"

They reached the trail entrance. He embraced his older sister.

He shook Werner's hand warmly. To them both, he said,

"I am proud that I have played a part. I always thought I was useless."

He turned and took the path that would take him over the hill, to Thedinghaus, to Havel, and then to Bremen.

He turned to wave a final good-bye.

"Things will be better -- that's what counts."

Twenty minutes later, Leo was wondering what Boston Harbor looked like when something hard as rock struck him on the back of the skull, and all went dark.

* * *

They say desert lizards feel the ocean tides.

Crustaceans burrow down into desert soils and hide in their shells when storms ravage the distant seas that were once their home. Elk and wild wolves synchronize their matings and migrations to the alliance between Moon and Ocean. The same with you and me, we mammals. We live and breathe in harmony with planetary currents in the unseen depths; some echo of those deep-sea canyons beneath Krakatoa are within us. Two hundred million tons of water move in and out of the Bay of Fundy each day: do you think that goes unnoticed? All living creatures respond to movements we cannot measure, in epic magnitudes we cannot gauge.

So it was that Leo awoke, knowing that something in the oceans below him was profoundly out of place.

Leo could hear the thrum of water – not a stream or a trickle but vast, fathomless expanses of living salt water. That was to be expected.

But as he rose, and sat on the edge of the cot, he was dimly conscious of some deeper currents running in the wrong directions.

He went to the cabin door, steadying himself as he walked.

He saw that he was on a frigate riding the swells of the mighty Atlantic Ocean under a brilliant blue sky.

The crewmen, seeing him up, called out below in a language he did not recognize.

All appears as it should appear, thought Leo. *And yet ...*

He looked up, into the impossible mass of moving clouds above the sails, against the blue. It was midday, and he could not see the stars --

"Good morning!" said the ship's Captain.

"My name is Tegethoff," said he. "How are you feeling -- "

"We're sailing south," said Leo, squinting up at the sky. "Not west."

The Captain shaded his eyes and joined his guest, scanning the brilliant blue sky, picking out

shifting shapes among the clouds. It was a new wind that blew, warm and fragrant, tousling their hair, filling the tall sails.

"You are yet bound for a new world, my Prince," said Tegethoff.

The ship yawed slightly as the sails caught and billowed with the force of the westerly breeze.

"It is not America, however."

The mast creaked.

"Africa."

* * *

Tergethoff, a practical, wry man, gave Leo free reign of the ship, even after Leo tried to escape and they fished him out of the Atlantic.

"You faux-rulers huddle in your castles," he said with a laugh one night over dinner.

"Who betrayed me?" demanded Leo.

"The House of Peenemude," replied the Captain. "Herr Melton."

"Your countrymen are switching to slaves," Tergethoff explained. "Better money.

"The House of Peenemude invested heavily in the African colony. Your family's name is on the original charter – your signature is needed.

"You'll sign a paper or two, and you're free," concluded Tergethoff.

Leo rattled the chains around his feet. He had his doubts. He would bide his time and wait for the opportunity to escape, once some kind of shore was near.

The *Rother Lowe* was a frigate, so the below-decks were minimal. She carried a cargo of guns in her hold, for tensions ran high with Gold Coast rivals Portugal and France; beating like war drums beneath that conflict was the simmering threat of native rebellion. Several brash chieftains had emerged among the tribes of Benin and the Ashanti, one of them speaking with dangerous eloquence of unification.

It was a different Leo who sailed around the Cape of Three Points and into the Gulf of Guinea, the morning of August 3. Long weeks at sea had hardened the young Brandenburg prince. Leo was half guest, half-prisoner, and he insisted on doing his share of deck work. He had added muscle to his shoulders and arm; stripped from him was a layer of boyhood romance about adventure. Still, he looked for a path to freedom.

Romy will be looking for me, Leo reminded himself.

My friends will come, if I can only get them word --

"Just the jibs, now!," called the Captain. "Look sharp, lads -- "

Coming into view was the settlement of Freidrichsburg, fenced fields and a huddle of grass structures and what looked like a wood fortress.

The deckhands of the *Rother Lowe* struck the mainsail. The frigate began its coast into the little harbor of impossibly clear, blue waters --

Leo's eyes scanned the banks, looking for a trail inland –

Here is my chance –

The ambush came with a sudden and overwhelming fury.

Lines of black-skinned archers appeared on the shore, brandishing arrows of flame.

The frigate's sails and decks caught fire as volley after volley rained down.

Canoes filled with shrieking banshees pulled alongside them. Nets were cast to hook onto the gunwales and the murderous mob clambered aboard --

Now the arrows were joined by flaming spears.

The war drums started up.

The crew of the *Rother Lowe* had no chance.

These are formal naval tactics, thought Leo, even as he ducked down into the holds, away from the fires and arrows –

We studied this. His mind cast up a vivid memory of Master Frestel, pacing among the desks ...

Ramses III did this against the Sea People--

The sable swarm moved forward with pace and discipline.

The melee devoured the European sailors.

Now the Africans advanced with long-bladed machetes, chucking bodies overboard as they did.

Sailors wailed for their families as they were hacked to a bloody death.

Tegetthoff was butchered only feet away from where Leo fought –

Leo picked up a sword and parried a foe. He skewered a second.

He toppled backward, betrayed by the chains around his ankles. Searching madly among the crates, Leo found the box of pistols he was looking for, mostly Sharpes and Duvals.

He turned and fired.

He felled one spear-wielding enemy, then whirled clumsily to strike down two more –

The Africans retreated, in some sort of rehearsed rotation --

Sun and Moon – thought Leo. *What devil has trained them --*

"Here are the guns!" cried Leo to the deckhands. "Grab a rifle! *Make a circle, boys.* We'll make a stand in the armory -- "

The German prince had hauled a heavy box of rifles to his shoulder when he was struck down from behind like a bowling pin.

He looked up from his back to see sharp spears looming over him --

"*Umukoro!*" called Leo. "I am a friend to Umukoro!" He showed the henna compass design on his wrist.

The spearmen paused.

They exchanged glances.

Leo heard stomping and shouting beyond, among the smoke and fire, on the doomed *Rother Lowe's* foredeck.

A tall, broad-shouldered man stepped out of the smoke.

He moved lithely, a figure from a dream, or some mist-shrouded common past. Keen-eyed, he did not need face paint or the lion markings on his shield to identify him as Warrior-King.

"*Well met, young Prince!*" said he, in perfect German.

"Does Dubin still tend his cabbages?"

A grin appeared on his face, white teeth shining against midnight-toned skin. He shattered the chains at Leo's feet, using the butt of a steel-forged knife.

"You're just the one we need," said Kamau Umukoru, scion of Oranmiyan, disciple of Kunle, chieftain of all the Edo.

The African Navigator.

His lusty laugh shook the strewn wooden crates. He reached out a chiseled arm to pull Leo to his feet --

"Come, brother! The girl-architect has been kidnapped. Yaa Asantewa calls! *A mighty war is afoot --* "

 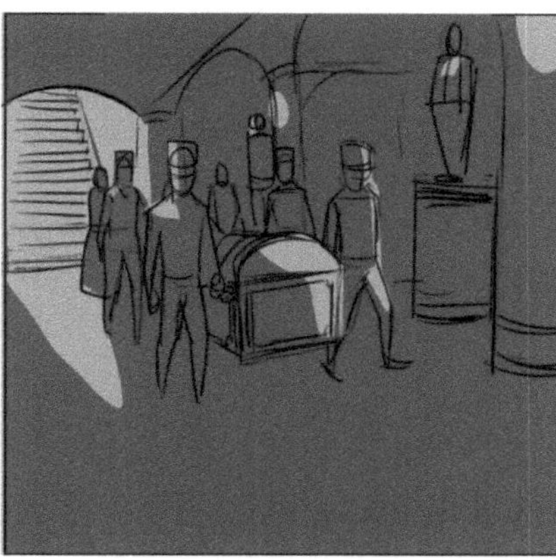 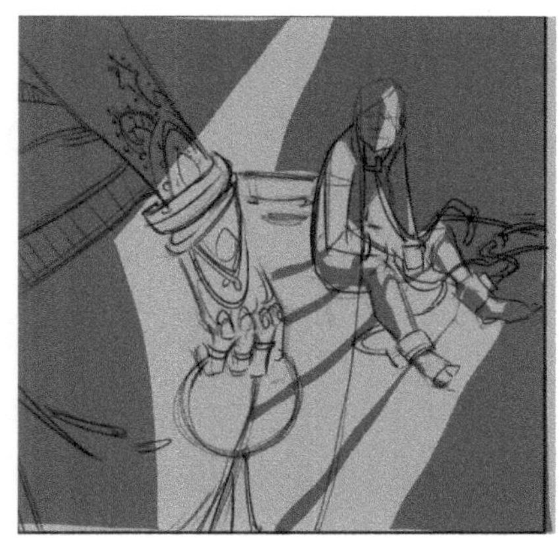

CHAPTER 16

Aftermath

Though much is taken, much abides.

-- Tennyson

"THRICE HAPPY," SAID DUBIN'S WIFE, trying to cheer him, but it was too soon, and he did not even look up from his work.

"How was your interview with the Josepha girl, dear? Is she French, or Levantine?"

"French," answered Dubin "We played chess."

He looked out at the gardens of the School for Young Monarchs. Waters ran contentedly through the irrigations streams which patterned the extensive gardens. A mother camel sauntered with her calf along the paths, headed for the orchard.

"They each played their parts, did they not?" said the wife.

"And paid a price for it," replied Dubin. "A wicked, wicked price. I did not warn them quite well enough about that."

"Will is not so bad off." She replied, careful in her tone of voice not to argue. "Sheyndil's letters sound positive. And Gilbert has found a mentor in General Washington. much acclaim. All France may change because of him."

"Jiayi Mei Ying -- "

"Is fighting a war that was coming for a decade. She loved her time here."

"And Leo fights beside Umukoru," she continued. "He has found the war he always sought -- "

There followed a gap, a silence filled with the sound of wind in the low branches of the trees, and a skitter from the monkeys. She left room for Mahmoud, the one he never mentioned.

"Come," she said at length. "Jara says she has a new letter from Cynthiana – she sends apple seeds -- "

The Schoolmaster rose and retrieved his gloves. He lifted the handles of the wheelbarrow.

He looked up at the sky, at its sweep and ever-changing components, as if trying to tell the future from its mood.

His wife looked up, too.

Out over the valley, at the fringe of the western horizon, a grouping of dark clouds gathered.

* * *

It was a pretty day on the Bosporus, bright white clouds rolling past, and the sky a jewel-like shade of blue.

Clean sunlight dappled the lush lawns visible from the open hallways of the Topkapi palace. Peacocks and camels strolled across the roads beyond the grass, and the waters of the Bosporus sparkled in the middle distance.

The marbled hallways of the fourth and innermost courtyard of the Topkapi Palace were calm. Sea breezes ruffled the long curtains along the quiet corridor. A pair of ostriches, hearing the tantrum, wandered over from the adjacent garden, and poked their snouts through the curtains.

The servant Yilmaz was on his knees on the polished stone floor, backing up, sweeping with his hand-broom and dustpan, when he bumped into someone.

"A thousand pardons -- "

He stopped.

He turned. Recognizing the face, he fell back.

"Yilmaz. What is it?"

The Sultan's daughter, Julide, appeared from a doorway.

She looked up and her hand fell over her mouth.

A pair of ostriches, hearing the tantrum, wandered over from the adjacent garden, and poked their snouts through the curtains.

By the time the Sultan's first wife, Bayazind, and her attendants arrived, Yilmaz was prostrate, feverishly reciting prayers for the dead, and the girl Julide was collapsed by one of the marble pillars, weeping.

"Kace! It's you, at las --" said Bayazind. She saw his face.

"*No!*" she cried. "Oh, no! No – no -- "

* * *

Yilmaz watched at the window.

In the private chamber, Kace held his audience rapt with attention.

He set the scene at Bemis Heights. He acted out the digging of trenches and construction of battlements. He paced off the distances and imitated the slow-footed Hessians, and played Gage's part in the great battle, and Arnold's, and Mahmoud's.

Standing on a sofa, the Cossack swept his arms to indicate the noble bravery which swept the American battlefield. He put an imaginary rifle to his shoulder, and his audience flinched at the imaginary gun's recoil, and watched with horror as he enacted how the British overran the colonial positions.

The women gasped at the final clash of hosts at Saratoga. They thrilled to hear Mahmoud's wise council to Horatio Gates, and asked Kace to speak the words clearly, and to describe Mahmoud's courage in battle, behind General Arnold, in detail.

They were surprised that Burgoyne did not use the Hessians.

Kace's small audience was shocked at Red Wolf's treachery.

They cheered Shooting Star, the Iroquois brave, and wept at seeing his death played out.

When they saw the treacherous actions of Taquin, they clenched their fists.

Purest silence filled the chamber when Kace showed how he held the fallen Prince, and how he tried to staunch the wound (but could not), and spoke again their final words.

His audience wept -- but happily so – upon hearing Kace recount the great victories that Prince Mahmoud had called into being.

They studied Kace's primitive drawings and asked him to repeat the drama again, which he did gladly.

He took out documents, letters of commendation from Gilbert, the Marquis de Lafayette, and the Colonial leader, Washington, and the good Daniel Morgan, and he read each of their warm remarks and commendations aloud.

Other attendants joined Yilmaz at the window, and followed the re-enactment, swaying and murmuring among themselves.

The long night stretched into the next day.

* * *

The procession moved slowly through the tombs.

Torches cast long and flickering shadows among the vast jumble of strange, towering forms as they passed. The priest chanted prayers.

"*There is no God but god,*" he said.

Mahmoud's second sister, Papatya, whose mind was slow, repeated the priest's chants in her own broken litany. The colossal tombs absorbed all these sounds.

The Prince's coffin moved into the lands of night, the lands of his ancestors.

A note was pinned to the scimitar which adorned the top of the coffin:

"*Apollo absent is Apollo still*" (in German).

The family passed giant chipped-tile wall mosaics of ancient Byzantium, depictions of the many civilizations which had contributed to the city's history.

"Our ancestors will rejoice to see you, Mamet," whispered Julide.

"*Allah u akbar,*" chanted the priest. "God is great."

The procession reached the family sepulcher.

* * *

Later that night, in the corridors of the palace, a beautiful young woman carried her sleeping child. The child, a boy, could not have been more than eight months old.

Bayazid stepped from the shadows.

She motioned for the woman's attendant to be gone. One hesitated, and was instantly strangled by two of the *streltsy* in Bayazid's company.

Sabahat, the newest wife of the Sultan, understood.

"Let me introduce you," said Bayazid in a voice of icy command.

"This is Taquin's wife. You hired her husband to kill my son. Had he failed, you would have killed her.

"And you know Julide." Revenge burned in those keen eyes. "Prince Mahmoud's sister. How she has grown!"

Kace stepped out of the shadows. He held a letter.

"What is that?" Sabahat clasped her hands so they would not tremble so.

"Taquin's will. And confession," answered Bayazid.

"What will happen to my son?" asked Sabahat.

"We will teach Cem all the lessons Mahmoud taught me," said Julide. "He will know the Latin names for all the animals."

She nodded in silence. Tears stained the dark markings around her eyes.

She handed the swaddled child to Julide.

Outside, the owl watched midnight descend on the palace grounds. The bird fell off the branch and swept low, wings wide, gliding, in patterns, over the moonlit grasses, hunting.

* * *

Sheyndil stood by the lamplight, by the tall window, in the longhouse, beneath the walls of shelves of seeds in jars, some glass, some ceramic, and read the letter again.

The lamp's warm light fell on the thick curtains, rendering a complex pattern, like a tapestry.

The new seeds had come in, with the stagecoach, cotton and carrot and more wheats and one jar marked "mouse-ear cress." Can you imagine.

A letter arrived, too.

Sheyndil opened and flexed the fingers of one hand, then the fingers of both hands.

The fires crackled and popped.

She ran her fingers over the paper, slowly, so she could take in the handwriting of each letter, each word.

Her shoulders heaved with her sobs, and when she could read no more she sat in the tall-backed, velvet-cushioned chair by the window and held her face in her hands, speaking his name again and again.

"*Mahmoud,*" she whispered. "Mahmoud. Mahmoud, *I'm so sorry...*"

CHAPTER 17

Consequences

After Saratoga, the Americans formed an alliance
with France that evened the military and naval
strengths, later bringing Spain
and the Dutch Republic into the conflict.

-- Rand McNally Atlas of History

MARCH 16, 1778

The ninth and final rule of war is this: Simplicity.

Prepare clear, uncomplicated plans and clear, concise orders to ensure thorough understanding.

Britain broke the Ninth Rule.

Britain's famously arrogant General Charles Cornwallis ("We'll go over and bag him in the morning," he said about Washington, the night before Trenton) needed food and ammunition so he could once and for all destroy the wicked Bostonians.

He had assembled twenty thousand men at Yorktown, their artillery was in place, their earthen-works dug, and he meant to pulverize the Continental Army and bury this revolution once and for all.

But Cornwallis needed food, and ammunition, so he sent for supplies to be delivered to him immediately, under the protection of the matchless Royal fleet.

Dutifully, a convoy of British warships with names like *Invincible* and *Monarch*, *Royal Oak* and *Resolution* and *Terrible*, conceited names which revealed the smug personality of the British naval force in general, sailed south serenely on this calm afternoon behind the flagship *HMS London* and entered along Chesapeake Bay to deliver Cornwallis' supplies.

Only to find the French Navy waiting for them.

Washington had summoned twenty-four French ships of the line up from the Caribbean, plus a squadron from Newport, and it was this sight that greeted the British fleet heavy with Cornwallis' bullets and grain and livestock.

The two sides engaged.

At the moment the British came head-to-head with the French, at the outset of the engagement, the British had the advantage of wind and position. But the British flagship, *London*, signaled that they would attack in the traditional manner, adopting formal tactics, tactics which prohibited all initiative. In so doing, the *Anglais* squandered their advantage. The British rear division never came into action.

It was not always visible, but there was a disease rotting the flesh beneath the British ships' gleaming surfaces, a cancer so pernicious that it had weakened the Royal Navy in ways that were not always apparent. This cancer had first taken hold in the branch's book-keeping, and spread to mismanagement in the Navy's civil administration, and thence to the ships themselves, and the men who sailed the, until all the Admiralty was at risk. From the moment the Earl of Sandwich was appointed Lord of the Admiralty, the cancers of embezzlement, larceny and swindling festered and grew in the dockyards. There was collusion between dockyard officials and ship-owners: the former would inspect and condemn vessels and the latter, having bought a ship, would change her name and appearance and sell her back to the government for transport service. The nation was charged with four thousand more men than were rated on the books of the Navy. For want of proper men to conduct the business of the ports, no effort was made to refit the ships. The dishonesty of the accountants and shipping agents and pursers soon entangled the admirals, some of whom participated in the fruits of embezzlement. Maltreatment of seamen, bad food, scurvy, incompetent medical services and other evils caused attrition among the sailors, who had no desire to serve on such wretched ships.

Young men with letters of introduction were promoted over officers who had earned their rank. "Politics has got too great a hold of the navy for me to withstand it," lamented one ship's captain in his letter of resignation. From the dockyards to the mastheads, England's Admiralty was corrupt.

And the cost was paid that afternoon on the blue waters of the Chesapeake.

The *Terrible*'s commanding officer, scion of a well-known and well-landed family, was too drunk to command. His Bosun took command, but this stubborn man was possessed of such a deep hatred of the French that he abandoned the overall good of the squadron and set upon the nearby *Villaret*. The two ships struck up a fierce fight. The *Terrible* struggled to escape, but her ragged rigging hindered her.

The battle lines converged amid constant cannon fire. The commanding officer of the *Monarch* took shelter under a turtle-shell deck which turned out to provide no protection whatsoever.

They melee raged as they sailed east, away from the bay.

The British ship *Royal Oak* was detached from the main squadron and pounded by the French sloop *Jacqueline*. Again and again, the French pilot thwarted the *Royal Oak*'s tack. Mauled in the close engagement, *Royal Oak* gave up, and retreated to the shoals of Maryland: her Captain was heard to shout, "I curse Columbus and all the discoverers of this Diabolical country."

The *London* ordered the *Anglais* fleet to execute a 180-degree turn, but the pilots of the *Monarch* and the *Resolute* were incompetent, and could not complete the command.

There was confusion among the British fleet's maneuvers, caused by apparently contradictory signals issued by the *London*.

Meanwhile, the *Terrible* and the *Villaret* clung together determinedly. The Bosun in charge of the English ship raised signals to the effect that he had hopes that if he stalled long enough, the elements would rise to claim the enemy. He was perhaps thinking in vain of the lucky storms which tipped the scales in the Scottish battle of the Spanish Armada. Paget, captain of the *Villaret*, was by contrast a lifelong sailor, a resourceful pilot who had played endless hours of sail-chase in his home-town harbor, Nice. Seeing that the supply-laden *Terrible* could not keep pace, he stayed to her leeward and blocked her every tack, raining down shell-fire all the while, snapping her mast in the second hour of the engagement. The *Terrible* was crippled, and she would sink to the bottom of the sea within a day.

The French flagship, *Lycee*, signaled a turn twenty degrees north, along the Maryland shore. As one, the French ships turned north.

The British ships, which had been in need of refitting even before the battle, followed suit, but in ragged order. The *Invincible* almost cashiered the *Monarch*: There was a continual raising and lowering of signal flags among the British ships, but the pace was so frenetic that the messages were misinterpreted, or missed altogether.

The stakes were clear: The English ships needed to drive away the French so he could land with Cornwallis' supplies: without them, Cornwallis could not fight. This was no random engagement: either defeat the French and land, or all was lost.

The French had mapped the winds of the Chesapeake cove, and knew that once they made it past the point at the bay's entrance, the wind shifted. At the *Lycee*'s signal, the French line abruptly jibed in unison: this violent maneuver almost snapped the ships' timbers, but the masts held, and momentarily the French sails popped with a full wind. The French line came running downwind at full tilt, every inch of canvas billowed, coming straight

towards the British formation. Amid much crunching of wood and shouting voices and firing of cannon and rifle and pistols, the French ships broke through the British line.

The British fell into disorder. Three of their ships were essentially lost to the engagement from that point forward, so ineffective were their commanders.

At dusk, after less than three hours' engagement, the firing ended.

The *London* gave a general signal to keep to windward: the heads of the two fleets separated.

The vaunted British Navy retreated.

They would not land in the Chesapeake Bay to deliver Cornwallis his supplies.

It was their lone defeat in two hundred years of dominance of the ocean seas.

Cornwallis, having neither bullets to fire or food to feed his soldiers, surrendered (too smug to surrender himself, he sent his second-in-command) two days later.

Combined, the French and American forces were too much for England.

The tide had turned.

The Colonials held the upper hand now.

They would not relent it.

CHAPTER 18

Balancing the Scales

Beware the fury of a patient man.

-- John Dryden

"NO! YOU CAN'T -- "

The girl tried to scream, but the thief cupped his rough hand over her mouth.

It was mid-morning, broad daylight in the remote village of Yavirnyk, among the snow-tinged Carpathian Mountains, above the rapids. The girl had come to the barn's penned-in corral to feed the cattle and goats and horses housed there.

A band of four thieves was raiding the village's livestock collective. They had waited for the men to leave on a hunting party. A score of the farm animals were already tied together, half of them were already out the gate. It would mean ruin, probable starvation for the *Zaporozhtsi* village.

"It's all we have," the desperate girl tried to say to the thieves, who were her own age.

The thieves' leader, Stepan, slapped her across the face once, and then slapped her again, harder, when she tried to struggle.

The girl did not cower, as they seemed to expect her to do. She managed to get to her feet. She seemed determined to stop them, or to raise an alarm.

Stepan took the girl and carried her into the barn, running his hands appreciatively over the fabric of her dress as he did. There would be just enough time to make her pay for her courage...

A creak of a hinge stopped him.

It was the barnyard gate opening.

Three gray-haired men stepped into the corral.

They were dressed in dark cloaks of thick fabric, hooded cloaks as you might see on a ship's deck. Two of them held Dutch military rifles, flint-locks, antiquated guns but, from the clean look of the barrels, in working order.

"It's him we want," said the short one in front of the other two, indicating the brigands' leader. "You others can go."

Stepan cocked his head. He directed his thieves to advance. Instantly, two of the old men let loose their muskets with a boom: two thieves fell instantly to the ground. They leveled their weapons at the third thief, who quickly slunk away. Stepan remained, hands raised.

"Stepan Kolyady," said one of the ancients.

"Who wants to -- "

The short one stepped forward and struck Stepan, with his open hand, much as Stepan had just done to the girl, but with far more force. Stepan fell to the ground. The ancient picked Stepan up and struck him again. He picked him up and struck him a third time. Now blood decorated the young thief's nose, and mouth, and a look of fear brightened his eyes.

"You worked in the shipyard of the Cossack, Kace."

Stepan blinked, still not understanding.

"In Constantinople. You beat an unarmed yard boy, almost to his death. A Turkish boy, with a tattoo like this."

The old man pushed back his sleeve: there, on the forearm, was a tattoo in faded hen and azure inks: it was of a compass.

Now Stepan faltered, and turned pale. Now he understood.

They had taken their time. It is important to be sure, in such matters. They had interviewed all the boys who had taken part in the moonlight beating in the Cossack's shipyard, the boy protected by the compass tattoo. They had been most deliberate in their investigations, and made meticulous inquiries until they were certain, and kept plainly-written records so their work could be seen by any who cared to know.

The flintlocks' shots had summoned a small crowd, mostly women. They did not interfere: Yavirnyk was not so far away from the sea that they did not know the Society of Navigators.

The old men conferred among themselves. One of them threw a rope over a tree by the barn, and with no more ceremony than that, they took revenge on Stepan the thief.

The old men's faces were long, and their speech was low as they fulfilled their part. They left a written account of Stepan's crime and their search for him, pinned to his vestments, a document with the seal of a mariner's compass, should any miss the meaning.

This had to mean something.

The three old men took their leave of the village of Yavirnyk, among the snow-tinged Carpathian Mountains, above the rapids. The girl embraced them, to their chagrin. Onlookers heard them speaking in Nederlander, or low Dutch, as heard sometimes in the Rhine valley also. Villagers recalled later that they mentioned the name Cynthiana, and the port of Boston, and the merits of a new instrument which purported to measure longitude.

CHAPTER 19

Mother's Visitors

Only a fool makes threats.
Only another fool feels threatened.

-- Paulo Coelho

MOTHER WAS STANDING AT THE rail by the long bench, looking out over the Flying Sand Weir, when the two visitors approached.

They wore city clothes, silk robes with sashes, big shoulders. Perfumed pomade kept their styled hair stiff.

It was the same spot where her daughter, Jiayi Mei Ying, had been the day of the visit from missionaries.

The lattices of the check gate of the bottle-necked portion of the river rippled as they conveyed clean water to irrigation channels, headed to southern fields. She watched the whirlpools spin off. Excess water was guided to the river's outer sections.

The tiles embedded in the long bench and its backsplash had been collected from ships, from artisans of many lands, some blue Dutch and some Confucian, some indigo and some gold-tipped, some Korean, some Japanese, some depicting

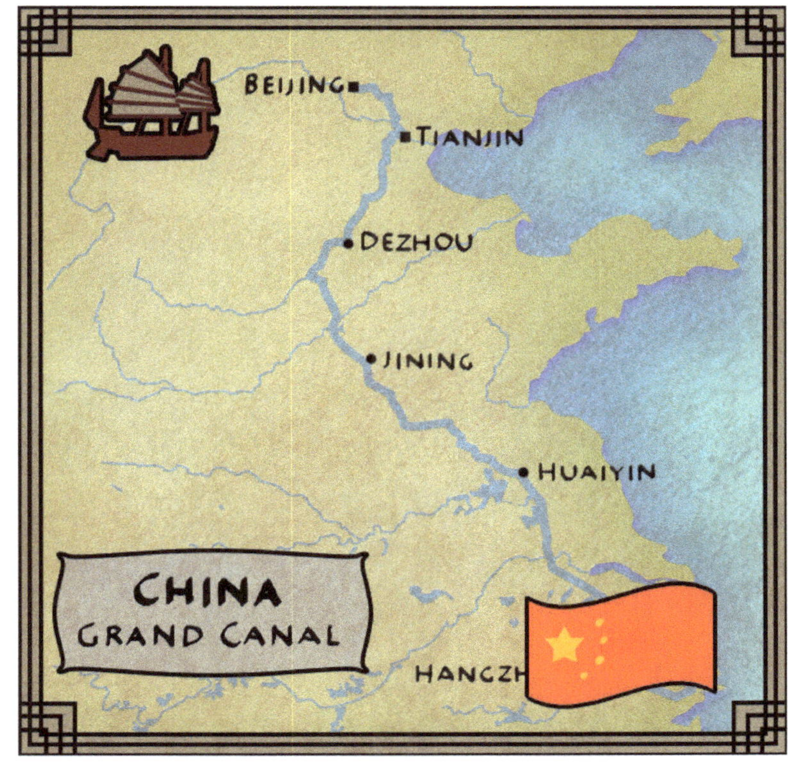

scenes of the Silk Road, depictions of great deeds, domestic scenes, celestial objects and birds in flight.

The two visitors stood in front of her ... a bit too close.

"We come with a message, Madame," said the first. "A warning. For the *Yunhe*. For the Peiken family."

"The new chamberlain has plans for the Ministry," said the first visitor coldly.

"Your domain is about to shrink. And radically."

Mother turned to face them fully.

"Stay out of our way and you may yet live out your years," said the smug city man.

"Sever your special ties to all the families whose lands touch the Canal.

"Your daughter – your reckless daughter, who brought about the death of not one but two of my two cousins – your daughter's presence in France is known to us. Our friends there may soon pay her a visit."

He placed his hand on the railing, reaching across Mother.

"What is your name, sir?"

"Pun Zihong."

"As in District Governor Zihong?"

"I am his brother."

"I see."

She tossed a pebble. It rolled neatly down the vertical slope, hopping on sandstone all the way to the Canal. It made a plopping sound when it entered the water.

"You wait until my husband is gone on his rounds.

"You come wearing wood-toothed shoes and silk sashes.

"You do not introduce yourself, neither do you use my title.

"And now you threaten my daughter's life ..."

The visitors failed to fully note the resolve in Mother's voice, and the arctic cold of her enmity.

She gripped the first man's wrist and arched her body, so that her full weight came to bear --

The man's wrist-bone snapped with a *Crack!*

He screamed and jumped in pain and surprise.

His momentum carried him over the rail.

"The *Yunhe* know no master --" she reminded him as he tumbled.

"Long live the Yunhe."

The second visitor was stocky, so she had to apply three strong blows to his neck before she could get his center of gravity clear of the railing. This one slid roughly down the sandy rockface head-first.

"Take these two to Lake Tai with you," called Mother to the sailors, who had been watching.

"Keelhaul them along the way."

"If they live, hold them in Zhiyu Bo's jail and let me know, I'll send a boat for them."

She glanced up at Grandfather, Ting Shen, Mother's father, who had been watching from his balcony.

He nodded.

It was war now.

Many a provincial lord, many an ambitious palace minister, many an Imperial ponce had come and gone since the Great Yu had signed the Peiken family's charter, and entrusted the Great Canal to them, and bestowed the nine tripod cauldrons. When Confucius was young.

Ever since, the family had remained loyal to the Emperor's purpose. Loyal, that is, to people of the *Yunhe*.

They had never wavered.

Mother put her hands on her waist, akimbo, and looked out over the waters of the Flying Sand Weir.

Waterborne vessels of every shape and size, ships and junks and schooners and rowboats, all moved briskly along the Emperor's great Canal. Here was cargo of wheat from Suzhou, medications from Ningbo all the way south to Beijing, in the north, ore and troops and farm equipment from Hebei produce and fabrics and perfume Luoyang, so far west that it touched the Silk Road. Commerce moved briskly to and from all points of China. The people depended on the *Yunhe* and its keepers for their daily lives, to build their homes and feed their families and keep them from disease. It was surely the engine of the Middle Kingdom.

Word of the keelhaulings would get out quickly.

This was an action that would set a cascade of events in motion.

Powerful new ideas were sweeping across the continents.

Mei Ying had lit the fuse.

The war had been coming for a long time.

Now these Western ideas of human rights and equality and justice for all swept the plains of the Middle Kingdom. Change, once gradual, was coming fast. The Bostonian ideals were taking hold, dug in deep, and news of each Colonial victory against foreign tyranny emboldened the people of the countryside. Mixing tribalism and fear of foreigners, avarice and superstition, tradition and modernity, this new transition would be complex and unpredictable, dangerous in ways local uprisings were not.

Behind Mother's figure, overlooking the Flying Sand Weir and its rippling waters, was the tiled bench. Its decorations spoke of many lands.

Behind and above the bench was a display case, as you might see in a museum. It was sturdy wood frame, several feet high and twelve feet long, mounted in stone and faced with a glass front.

Inside the wide and shallow encasement, lit by a flame, sat nine tripod cauldrons, forged in iron. They were symbols of the Water Keepers' permanent Imperial charge, the *Yunhe's* everlasting bond to and authority over the Canal, and all its waters and associated borderlands, all its commerce and all its doings, the ships which sailed it and the men who sailed the ships.

Mother rolled up her sleeves.

For China. For the people of China.

Her slim arms were not corded, like Father's, nor scarred from combat. Yet their grip on the hilt of the long-blade was unshakable.

Let the riders come.

Epilogue

Having now finished the work assigned me,
I retire from the great theatre of Action.

-- George Washington, in his farewell to Congress

DECEMBER 15, 1824, COLUMBIAN COLLEGE *commencement, Washington D.C.*

"Has it been so long?" roared Marie-Joseph Paul Yves Roch Gilbert du Motier, Marquis de Lafayette.

The crowd of young people roared back, cheering him ardently. Lafayette was a figure from myth, a hero warrior from the Revolution standing at the first commencement of the college George Washington imagined,

"Has it been forty years, *mes amis?*"

Another cheer.

"Foggy Bottom never looked so good," he said. "Over there -- " he pointed to a row of dormitories, "that was Rock Creek. Fit only for snakes. And there," he pointed behind the crowd, "the soldiers of the 18th Brigade set up their brewery." He shook his head. "Now it looks like Philadelphia." 

"So much has happened since I was last in America," Lafayette told the audience. "The freedoms that we fought for at Brandywine have spread far and wide." He looked around the gathering, from side to side. "But then, you knew I would say that."

The lines around his eyes had deepened, but the eyes themselves had lost none of their lively intelligence. The hair that tumbled over his collar was gray. His voice – the voice was different.

"President Monroe has promised a blanket of protection reaching Simon Bolivar, and San Martin and O'Higgins, from Havana to the tip of Tierra del Fuego.

"Now you have added Missouri to the Union. The twenty-fourth state. *Ma fois!* Twenty-four! How is that possible? How many will you have, in the end? Thirty? Forty?

"Far from our little gathering, today, a new nation rises. A State of freed slaves. Liberia. As we sit here, a continent away the Ashanti fight for their freedom, as do the Burmese, *two* continents hence.

"This ... all this ... is General Washington's dream. *You* are General Washington's dream. He left fifty shares in the Potomac Company as your first endowment. Fifty shares. He imagined a school to prepare smart, fearless government leaders, leaders who understood the international design, leaders to shine the bright light of liberty wherever there is darkness in the affairs of men.

"That is you.

"Now I have a son," said Gilbert. "He is your age. He will grow up in a world that the General hoped for."

"The stories you have heard about the War – are true. Some. But those are the easy stories to tell. The full account is much wider, and much deeper, and harder to grasp. I struggle with it myself, piecing it all together.

"You need to know," said the Marquis, placing his notes aside, "about three young people – just your age –without whom we would have failed. They made the Bostonian cause an international war, fighting Britain's empire on all front, all seas.

"They were my friends.

"The first was a young Russian woman who risked her life to support the Colonial cause. A jewess named Shay. Sheyndil Czarlinsky. She wrote the declaration of neutrality for Catherine the Great. She helped printers and writers spread the words and ideas of the Colonial cause to all Asia; she eliminated assassins and traitors who wanted to keep Russian oligarchs in power. It was her pact, her vision that bound the internationals together.

"The second was a Dutch trader. His name was Will Oldenbarnevelt. He led a group of Dutch merchants to underwrite the Americans; it was his personal loan guarantee – at the risk of his family's fortune – that pushed Louis the Sixteenth to enter the war. An unwritten rule of war is that the side with more money usually wins. Lord North ran out of money, but the Colonial cause scraped by. Always, just scraped by. Thanks to the Dutch merchants.

"The third was a Turkish prince. His name was Mahmoud. He pledged the Ottoman Navy to join in the American cause. He signed a treaty, turning his people away from war with Russia, so both nations could oppose Britain all across the world. He gave his life to deliver these letters to me, and to General Washington, at Valley Forge, so we could sway Congress. Mahmoud gave his life at Saratoga. He would have become the greatest Sultan of his century, had he lived.

"You owe them!" said Lafayette. "You walk in their footsteps.

"Earn it!" concluded the Marquis de Lafayette.

"Earn it!" the crowd roared.

Author Bio

Tom Durwood is a teacher, writer and editor with an interest in history. Tom most recently taught English Composition and Empire and Literature at Valley Forge Military College, where he won the *Teacher of the Year* Award five times. Tom has taught Public Speaking and Basic Communications as guest lecturer for the Naval Special Warfare Development Group at the Dam's Neck Annex of the Naval War College.

Tom's ebook *Empire and Literature* matches global works of film and fiction to specific quadrants of empire, finding surprising parallels. Literature, film, art and architecture are viewed against the rise and fall of empire. In a foreword to *Empire and Literature*, postcolonial scholar Dipesh Chakrabarty of the University of Chicago calls it "imaginative and innovative." Prof. Chakrabarty writes that "Durwood has given us a thought-provoking introduction to the humanities." Tom's subsequent book "Kid Lit: An Introduction to Literary Criticism" has been well-reviewed. "My favorite nonfiction book of the year," writes The Literary Apothecary (Goodreads).

Early reader response to Tom's historical fiction adventures has been promising. "A true pleasure ... the richness of the layers of Tom's novel is compelling," writes Fatima Sharrafedine in her foreword to "The Illustrated Boatman's Daughter." The Midwest Book Review calls that same adventure "uniformly gripping and educational ... pairing action and adventure with social issues." Adds Prairie Review, "A deeply intriguing, ambitious historical fiction series."

Tom briefly ran his own children's book imprint, Calico Books (Contemporary Books, Chicago). Tom's newspaper column "Shelter" appeared in the *North County Times* for seven years. Tom earned a Masters in English Literature in San Diego, where he also served as Executive Director of San Diego Habitat for Humanity.